"Am I decorous and submissive enough?"

Marina's eyes flashed at him defiantly as she spoke.

"No matter what you wear you always look provocative," Vittorio murmured as his glance went to her mouth, lingering there deliberately. His lips parted and he licked them with the tip of his tongue, as if he were either hungry or thirsty.

"Don't you mean sexy and silly?" Marina whispered. Her senses were suddenly very much alive. But seeing him, scenting his masculinity, hearing the musical intonations of his voice wasn't enough. She wanted to feel the pressure of his lips, the touch of his fingertips.

"Sexy, but not silly. Never silly," he replied, stepping even closer, so that now there was no space left between them at all.

FLORA KIDD

dark seduction

Harlequin Books

TORONTO • NEW YORK • LOS ANGELES • LONDON
AMSTERDAM • PARIS • SYDNEY • HAMBURG
STOCKHOLM • ATHENS • TOKYO • MILAN

Harlequin Presents first edition May 1983
ISBN 0-373-10592-4

Original hardcover edition published in 1983
by Mills & Boon Limited

CHAPTER ONE

'VITTORIO MATISSI,' Marina Gregson repeated the name slowly and thoughtfully, giving no hint that she recognised it. 'He sounds Italian to me,' she added.

'He's from Sicily,' replied Sylvia Trent crisply. The owner and manageress of the model agency, she had been a leading fashion model herself over twenty years ago, and her figure was still trim and her dark brown hair showed no sign of grey. Only about the eyes, mouth and in her long thin hands did her age show.

'A member of the Mafia?' said Marina brightly and almost flippantly, her lips curving into the mischievously mysterious smile which had appeared often on the cover of a well-known international fashion magazine. She had always had a tendency to be flippant or to make jokes when she was seriously and deeply disturbed.

'How would I know?' retorted Sylvia. 'All I can tell you is that he's in the fruit exporting business and his company has an office in London.'

'What does he want a model for?' asked Marina. 'To advertise his fruit?'

'He didn't say why. He gave me a description of you and produced an old copy of *Charm* magazine with you on the cover. Actually it was the December copy of the year before last—the edition which came out just before you were in that accident. You were modelling a very sexy evening gown.'

'I remember,' Marina murmured. It had been the last time she had modelled for *Charm*.

'Anyway, this Vittorio Matissi said that if I could find you he would like to interview you ... at least I assumed he wants to interview you,' Sylvia continued.

'When?'

'Today, if possible. That's why I asked you to come into town. If you're agreeable I've to phone him immediately and he'll tell me where and when he'll meet you.'

Marina stared unseeingly at the wall behind Sylvia's desk. It was decorated with blown-up photos of some of the models Sylvia had groomed and coached and sent on to stardom of one sort or another. Once her photograph had been there among them. Now, it was missing.

'Well? Shall I call Mr Matissi and tell him you'll meet him?' Sylvia spoke crisply and coolly, bringing Marina back to the present, forcing her to make a decision.

'No, I don't want to meet him. I ... I ... well, I don't like the sound of him. What else is there?' she asked.

'Nothing,' replied Sylvia flatly.

'Oh, come on, there must be something,' said Marina coaxingly.

'I could fix you up with a few hours' modelling for an advertising agency which does copy for a department store or even for a fashion show in the same department store. Or how about modelling in the nude for the life drawing class at a college of art?'

'No, thanks!' Marina made a little grimace of distaste, then with an effort she dropped the barrier of her pride and asked, 'Doesn't Marius want me back? He should be putting on his Paris show of his Spring collection in a few weeks' time. And what about *Charm*? Kaye Burnett, the art editor, liked those covers I did for them and said she'd like me to do more. Have you been in touch with her and told her I'm available to model again?'

'I've been in touch with everyone,' said Sylvia with a sigh. For a moment she studied Marina, her brown eyes softening with sympathy. 'Look, you're going to have to face up to reality, Marina, and it may as well be today as tomorrow. Since you dropped out of the fashion model scene fourteen months ago plenty of new models have come along. New faces, young faces, girls who don't limp when they walk.'

'But I don't limp,' retorted Marina forcibly, sitting up straight, but under her make-up her face went white.

'You may think you don't, but it's noticeable that you don't walk with the grace you used to walk with—and you know Marius, he has to have the best models. There mustn't be a blemish anywhere.' Sylvia sighed again. 'I hate to have to say this, but you're never going to be a top model again. You've had it.' She spoke with cold finality, but her eyes still brimmed with sympathy.

'Thank you,' replied Marina proudly. 'Thank you for telling me I've wasted my time coming here.' She rose to her feet. 'There are other agencies.' She stalked to the door of the office.

'Now, wait a moment. Don't go off half-cocked,' said Sylvia, standing up and going round the end of her desk. 'I've been cruel to be kind, don't you see that? Until you face the fact that you're right back where you started over four years ago when you began to model and that it's going to be a long hard pull to get back into even fourth or third position, you're not going to get any sort of modelling job.' She stepped closer to Marina. 'I like you and I always have. You've a lot of pride and spirit, and it was a near-tragedy you were involved in that car crash. But I wouldn't like you to go downhill just because you're no longer in demand as a top model. There are plenty of other things in life to do.'

'Such as?' Marina challenged her chin up. 'I'm not trained to do anything else but modelling and I need a job immediately. My savings are all used up.'

'Why don't you find out at the employment exchange what sort of re-training programmes they have for women these days?' suggested Sylvia practically. 'But before you do that, go and meet this Mr Matissi and find out what he has in mind. He assured me that the suggestion he's going to make to you is all above board and quite legal.' Sylvia's mouth curled wryly. 'I had to question him closely to make sure he wasn't in the white slave traffic or something like that! Or that he

wasn't looking for a pillow-mate for the duration
of his stay in London. Shall I phone him? You
never know, it might be a good opportunity.'

Marina nibbled her lower lip. If she didn't go
and meet Vittorio Matissi what would she do
instead? Go to the other modelling agencies and be
told the same story Sylvia had told her? Go to the
employment exchange and sign on with hundreds
of other people who were looking for jobs in this
period of economic depression? Or should she take
one of the part-time modelling jobs Sylvia had
offered? Or should she go back to the small flat
she was sharing with a friend and mope about,
sinking slowly into the slough of self-pity?

She looked out of the window. The sky was
heavy and grey. It looked as if it might snow.
According to the weather records the winter that
was almost over had been the worst for more than
thirty years, and now at the end of March one
would have expected some sunshine. But no;
outside it was cold and blustery. She was tired of
being cold, tired of bad weather. She longed
suddenly for hot sunshine pouring like molten
gold out of a brilliant blue sky. She longed for
yellow sands, sparkling blue-green water, wind-
tossed palms . . .

'All right. Phone Matissi and tell him I'll meet
him,' she said, turning to smile at Sylvia. 'No one
will ever say I wouldn't take a chance!'

'That's better. That's more like you,' said Sylvia,
her face lighting up with an expression of relief
and, going over to her desk, she picked up the
phone and began to dial a number.

An hour and a half later Marina dropped off a red double-decker bus in Piccadilly. Wearing an attractive mock-fur coat, high black boots and a cossack-style fur hat perched on top of her long silvery blonde hair, she stepped carefully along the wet pavement, weaving her way through narrow West End streets until she reached the entrance of an exclusive restaurant.

A commissionaire opened the door for her. Inside she was greeted by another uniformed official. The atmosphere of the foyer was warm and luxurious. It was an elegant, quiet haven from the dreary weather outside.

'May I help you, miss?'

'I'm meeting a . . . a Signor Matissi here. Has he come yet?'

'Your name, miss?'

'Marina Gregson.'

'Signor Matissi is waiting for you, in the second alcove on the right. The cloakroom is on the left as you go towards the steps. The attendant there will be pleased to take your coat.'

The carpet was thick and a soft shade of pink. It was decorated with a flower pattern in pale gold and green. Marina left the fur coat and hat in the cloakroom. A glance in a mirror assured her that the silvery green suit she was wearing was a good choice because its simple straight skirt and long-lapelled fitted jacket worn over a blouse of white lace flattered her slim figure. She returned to the foyer, aware of pale pink walls and gilt lighting fixtures, and went up the steps. Walking slowly, her head up and her shoulders back, she moved along a wide hallway which had alcoves opening off it on either side. There was only the slightest stiffness in the movement of her left leg.

In the second alcove on the right a man was sitting on the curved cushioned seat behind the oval glass-topped coffee table. His head was tipped back against the back of the couch and his eyes were closed. He was dressed in a dark navy blue suit, and a white shirt with a red silk tie patterned with small white diamond shapes. On the table in front of him was a cut glass tumbler containing some gold-coloured liquid. Beside it was a thick magazine with a glossy cover. Marina could see that a photograph of herself wearing a red evening dress was on the cover.

She cleared her throat loudly. His eyelids lifted and he looked right at her with dark brown eyes. Not a muscle of his face moved and it seemed to her that he stared at her far too long.

'Signor Matissi?' she queried pleasantly, stepping forward and holding out her right hand. 'I'm Marina Gregson.'

He rose to his feet. Standing, he was about three inches taller than she was, and in her high-heeled boots she was five feet nine. Under the well-cut double-breasted suit jacket his shoulders were wide—too wide, it seemed to her, for the jacket. He was a muscular tough with a swarthy sun-tanned square-jawed face and elegantly cut jet-black hair, and he was dressed in a suit that could only have been tailored in the West End of London. He oozed power, plus elegance, and for a few moments, she found him overwhelming.

'I am pleased to meet you,' he said with bland politeness, shaking her hand. His voice was musical and resonant. It made her think of places where the sun shone warmly. He spoke English with only the slightest of accents. 'Thank you for coming at such short notice,' he added. 'Please sit down.'

She slid along the cushioned seat of the couch until she was facing him across the table. A waiter appeared.

'What would you like to drink?' Vittorio Matissi asked her.

'I thought this was to be an interview,' she replied cautiously.

'That is no reason why we shouldn't enjoy good food and drink while we are talking. May I suggest sherry or vermouth?'

Marina chose a sweet vermouth. He ordered and the waiter went away after leaving two menus with them. Vittorio Matissi leaned back and finished drinking what was in his glass, then he set the empty glass down and looked across at her. His eyes which were large and heavy-lidded were wide open, their expression hard and cold in spite of their velvety dark brown colour.

'You look exactly as I expected you to look from the descriptions Francesco gave me,' he said. He pointed to the magazine, where from the shiny cover her own face smiled up at Marina. 'That photograph doesn't do you justice. You look ... how shall I put it?' He snapped a finger and thumb together. 'Sexy but silly,' he added.

'Well! Thank you for nothing!' exclaimed

Marina, and he grinned suddenly, showing perfectly shaped large white teeth. The flash of whiteness transformed his dark face, giving a hint that he wasn't always the suave businessman; that there was a lighter side to his nature which was not, perhaps, often on show.

'Now I've offended you,' he said, and gestured with big muscular hands. 'It was always thus. I say what I think and it gets me into trouble, especially with the women in my family. I meant to say that it is only on meeting you like this, face to face, do I see what Francesco saw in you. It doesn't show in the photograph.' He flicked the magazine with a scornful finger.

'Francesco?' repeated Marina cautiously. 'You did say Francesco, didn't you?'

'I did. Francesco Barberini.' He leaned forward. The humour had gone from his face as swiftly as it had come, and his dark eyes gleamed coldly. 'Does the name strike a chord, Miss Gregson?' he asked softly. 'Or have you swept the memory of the young Sicilian who fell in love with you more than a year ago right out of your mind?'

'No, no, of course I haven't. I've often wondered about Frankie,' she protested. 'How is he?'

'Not very resigned to his present condition, right now. Unlike you, he can't walk.'

'Oh!' She was shocked. 'I'm sorry, so very sorry,' she whispered.

'You say that as if you mean it.' His broad-lipped mouth curled cynically.

'I do mean it.'

'Yet you haven't communicated with him since the car crash,' he accused her.

'It was difficult . . . I mean, it has been difficult for me,' she replied. 'I was in a coma for a while after the crash, and by the time I'd recovered and was well enough to ask for Frankie he'd gone. He'd been taken away from the hospital. I was told that he'd been transferred by his relatives to a hospital in Switzerland where he could receive the best treatment.' She paused, because the waiter had appeared with their drinks. The glass of vermouth was set before her and another glass of whisky and water was set before Vittorio Matissi. The waiter went away.

'That is true. I arranged for Francesco to be moved from the hospital in Kent where you were both taken after the crash,' said Vittorio Matissi smoothly.

'I remember he was expecting you,' said Marina. 'And that was why . . .' She broke off abruptly and picking up the glass of vermouth drank some of the liquid quickly.

'Go on, Miss Gregson, please. You were saying Francesco was expecting me to arrive in London and that was why he . . . what?'

She glanced at him uneasily. With his swarthy complexion, crisply waving black hair and slightly hooked nose he had a rather devilish appearance, and she didn't like that ironic curl to his lips or the dangerous narrowing of his eyes. She drank some more vermouth and said vaguely,

'I really don't remember everything that happened before the crash.' If Vittorio Matissi had

had the impression that she was silly before he had even met her she was about to convince him now that his impression had been right. 'We'd been to a New Year's Eve party, you know,' she went on with a little laugh. 'And we were . . . well, a little lightheaded and lighthearted.'

'Meaning you'd both had too much to drink, I suppose,' he remarked dryly. He curled long fingers flecked with black hairs about the glass of whisky and raised it to his lips. He drank slowly, his dark glance never leaving her face. Trying to hold on to her poise in the face of his provocative insolence, Marina drank some more vermouth.

'Francesco was eloping with you,' Vittorio announced abruptly. 'He was taking you to France and he was going to marry you there. He was doing it to defy his grandfather, Giovanni Barberini.' His lips curled again, even more scornfully. 'I'm sure you know, because I suspect he told you, that Francesco is the heir to a substantial fortune. One of these days he'll be one of the richest men in this part of the world.'

'I met him only a few times,' replied Marina stiffly. 'And at the time I was engaged to someone else, so I never thought of marrying Frankie. I was not eloping with him.'

'Do you deny then that he suggested marriage to you?' he queried, raising his eyebrows in surprise.

'No, I can't deny that. He did suggest marriage. But I thought he was joking. I'd told him that I was going to marry Steve,' she replied.

'Was this Steve you talk about at the party?'

'Yes, he was.'

'Then why did you go with Frankie when the party was over? Why didn't you go with Steve?'

Marina was silent, staring at the dregs of vermouth in her glass, her fingers fiddling nervously with the stem of the glass. In the liquid she seemed to see again Steve with Anne Collins, one of her modelling friends. Steve with his arms about Anne. Steve kissing Anne. Again she felt the hurt bewilderment she had experienced at the party when she had realised that Steve, to whom she had been engaged to be married for six months, had preferred Anne to herself. There had been only one way to assuage the pain. She had drunk too much and had found comfort in the worshipping gaze and caresses of Frankie Barberini.

'I don't have to answer your questions, Signor Matissi,' she said coldly. 'I'm not on trial for doing something wrong.'

His glance went to her left hand which was playing with the vermouth glass.

'You're not wearing a wedding ring. Does that mean you're not married to Steve?' he asked.

'I'm not married to him, nor am I likely to be married to him,' she snapped irritably. 'He's married someone else.'

'So?' His eyebrows tilted again, this time rather derisively. 'Then do you have a lover at the present time?'

'Oh, really!' Marina rose instantly to her feet. She had had quite enough of Signor Vittorio Matissi.

'Where are you going?' he demanded, also rising to his feet.

'I'm not staying any longer to answer your insolent questions about my personal life! You and I have nothing more to say to each other. Thank you for inviting me here, but I'm no longer interested in anything you have to say or any offer of a position you have to offer,' she snapped between her teeth.

She didn't see him move, but by the time she had edged by the coffee table he was beside her, preventing her from leaving. She could have sat down and slid around the curving couch, but she guessed that by the time she did he would be waiting there, cutting off her escape, and they would become engaged in some farcical game of cat and mouse. Facing him as calmly as she could, she looked up directly into his eyes.

'Please will you step aside,' she said haughtily. 'I would like to leave, Signor Matissi.'

'And I would like you to stay, Miss Gregson,' he replied, his mouth twitching slightly as if he wanted to grin. 'To have lunch with me, *per favore.*'

Marina held herself stiffly, her lids drooping down over her eyes as she realised he was looking at her in a way that had the effect of turning her knees to jelly. That warm glow in those dark eyes must have charmed more than one woman, she warned herself, inviting her to her downfall.

'I don't want any lunch if it's going to be bought by you,' she retorted as insultingly as she could. She raised her eyelids and braved the glance again. 'I've no wish to be under any obligation to anyone who's as rude and overbearing as you are!'

The warm glow faded. Something wicked sparked in his eyes and for a moment she knew fear; fear of a man, something she had never experienced before.

'Sit down, Miss Gregson,' he purred, moving closer to her until he was just touching her and she was forced to move back and sit down. Immediately he sat beside her. He picked up the menu, opened it and placed it before her. 'Don't hesitate to choose what you like,' he said in a voice as smooth as silk. 'Regardless of expense. I'm told that smoked salmon is an English delicacy which has to be tasted to be believed. Would you care to start the meal with some?'

Fear still flickering through her, acutely aware of the taut muscularity of his arm as it brushed against hers and of his thigh as it pressed along her thigh, Marina looked at the menu. Smoked salmon cost more than she would usually pay for a whole meal at a restaurant where she ate sometimes with friends. She glanced sideways at Vittorio Matissi and found he was watching her out of the corners of his eyes from under drooping lids. A faint ironic smile curled the corner of his lips.

He wasn't going to let her leave easily, and she didn't want to risk making a scene in front of the waiter, who had reappeared. She would have to stay and eat with this arrogant man who was daring to laugh at her secretly. One hand clenched on her knee and she found she was grinding her teeth in anger. But caution prevailed. She might as well make him pay handsomely for the privilege of having her company.

'Yes, I would like smoked salmon,' she replied serenely as if they had never clashed. 'I've never eaten it before.'

'Then it will be a new experience for both of us, one we'll share together,' he said smoothly. 'And to follow—the lobster or some roast beef?'

She chose roast beef, he gave the order to the waiter without referring to her again, choosing the wine without consulting her about her preference. Then they followed the waiter up some more steps and into a wide long dining room where they were shown to a table near a window which overlooked a small walled garden. Above the wall the top of a bus could be seen going by, its bright red a cheerful contrast to the grey wall and the slanting grey rain.

Marina sat down and looked around. Mostly men were sitting at the other tables, businessmen in dark suits. The few women in the room were elegantly dressed in model suits or dresses. No one looked poor.

Two young waiters approached the table. Behind them hovered an older waiter, watching everything they did. They set down plates of smoked salmon, flakes of golden-pink fish to be eaten with tiny wedges of brown bread and butter. White wine was poured from a long-necked bottle into glasses and the bottle was placed in an ice bucket on a small trolley beside the table. Vittorio Matissi offered bread to Marina. She took some and they both began to eat. After a while he asked,

'Do you like the salmon?'

'It's different,' she replied, not sure whether she liked the salty, smoke-tangy taste.

'I could say you're different and you could say I'm different,' he said mockingly. 'Each of us is different from the other. Not only are we of different sexes but we have different origins, come from different countries, have had different upbringings. Perhaps smoked salmon is an acquired taste, one you or I could become accustomed to if we ate enough of it. Do you think you and I could learn to like each other if we saw enough of each other?'

Marina gave him a slow scathing glance from under her long curling lashes, suspecting he was making a pass at her. There was a glint of amusement in his dark eyes.

'I can't answer your question because I don't know anything at all about you,' she replied coolly.

'Then—Frankie didn't tell you anything.'

'Apart from telling me he was expecting you he said nothing about you.'

'Then I must fill you in,' he said, the mocking curve to his mouth becoming more pronounced. 'I'm thirty-five years of age, I'm not married and I'm the only surviving male member of the Matissi family. At the present time I am the marketing director of the Matissi Company which exports fruits and vegetables from Sicily to this country and to other European countries—you may have seen the name on crates of oranges in your markets. As you might imagine, I travel a lot in Europe. I come to London often. Last year when I was coming to this country my eldest sister, Lucia Barberini, asked me to look up her son Francesco, who was attending an English university to study English Language as well as Economics and Business Management. He had not been home to Sicily for Christmas and she was worried about him.'

He stopped speaking to finish eating the salmon on his plate. Then he laid down his knife and fork, wiped his mouth on the table napkin and picked up his wine glass.

'I wrote to Frankie to tell him I was coming to see him. I know he received the letter, because you have just told me he told you he was expecting me,' he continued, drank some wine and set his glass down. He stared at her narrowly. 'Do you know why my sister was worried about Frankie?'

'No. He never talked about his family to me. I've told you I met him only a few times. Why was she worried?'

'He had written to her, just before Christmas, to tell her he had met you and fallen in love with you and intended to marry you. He sent her that copy of the magazine I showed you so that she would see what you look like. My sister panicked and asked me to see Francesco and persuade him to return home and to drop his affair with you before his grandfather heard about it.' His mouth tightened and he frowned. 'Francesco guessed why I wanted to see him, so he cut and run before I was able to meet him.' He gave her a hard penetrating glance across the table. 'He eloped with you.'

'But I've told you, we weren't eloping,' she protested. 'At least, I wasn't. Frankie offered to drive me home from the party. It was very foggy and . . .' She broke off as the memory of the crash surged into her mind. 'You know what happened,' she whispered.

'Yes, I know,' he murmured. 'There was a railway bridge over the road along which Frankie was driving. He was going too fast for the conditions. He didn't see the curve in the road where it went under the bridge and he drove straight into one of the stone pillars supporting the bridge. The car was a write-off. You were both lucky to survive.' His voice was flat emotionless. 'You lived in London then, didn't you?'

'Yes.' Marina looked at him sharply. He was still staring at her, his eyes slitted thoughtfully.

'Yet Frankie wasn't driving towards London,' he said.

'Then where was he going?' she exclaimed.

'In the opposite direction, towards the Kentish coast, to Dover and France. He told me and later his mother that he was hoping to marry you there.'

'I didn't know,' she muttered, shaking her head so that the fluffy blonde waves shimmered across her head. 'He didn't say anything. I ... I really believed he was taking me home. I didn't know he was serious.'

'He's still serious,' he said with a touch of scorn. 'He still wants to marry you, and he asked me to look for you while I was in London this time. He said he didn't know where you lived or even where your family lives, and he asked me to give you this if I should find you.'

He slipped his hand inside the lapel of his jacket and took an envelope from the inside pocket. Marina took the letter from him and stared down at Frankie's writing while the waiters cleared away empty plates and set the places for the next course.

'I'll read it later,' said Marina, putting the letter in her slim, envelope-shaped handbag.

'No—now, if you please. It's an invitation, and I'd like to know if you're going to accept it or refuse it before we finish lunch. Then I'll know what to tell my sister when I phone her this evening.'

'Oh, very well,' she said rather ungraciously, and picked up the letter again.

There were three pages of thick paper closely written on one side only and she couldn't absorb all of it at that first swift reading, but she had the impression that Frankie had thought of her often during the past few months and had longed to have news of her. He ended the letter by saying how much he loved her and how he hoped she would fly out to stay with him at his island home off the coast of Sicily.

'I would like you to stay as long as you wish,' he had written. 'And I am sure that when I see you again the desire to walk will return to my legs. My mother asks me to entreat you to come as she wishes very much to meet you. Please come, Marina.'

She folded the pages and pushed them back into the envelope. The waiter asked her how she liked her beef carved. She answered him and watched the slices of juicy reddish-brown meat fall away from the roast as the knife sliced through it. She was touched by Frankie's letter. It made her feel good to know that he had not forgotten her after all.

'So what is your answer?' Vittorio Matissi's voice was sharp and demanding. Marina looked across at him again. 'Will you accept Frankie's invitation and visit him on Biscari? He isn't able to travel far yet, so he can't come and see you.'

'Is Biscari far from the mainland of Sicily?' she asked, stalling for time, not wanting to rush into committing herself until she knew more.

'About thirty miles off the eastern coast. The Barberini family comes from there.' He leaned back in his chair as the waiter served him. 'Didn't Frankie tell you anything about his family?' he asked, looking rather puzzled.

'No. We talked mostly about the things he was interested in here in London, about the theatre, films and music. What is his family's business?'

'Handling and shipping freight. Barberini means container ships. Giovanni Barberini's father started the business moving cargo between Sicily and other parts of the Mediterranean. Now it is a world-wide business. Giovanni is still alive and it is already known that he considers Frankie his heir since his own son ... my sister's late husband ... died a few years ago. Naturally Giovanni is suspicious of any woman who attracts Frankie's interest. He doesn't want his heir being married for the money he will one day inherit.'

'I see,' murmured Marina. 'He's afraid of fortune-hunters and he suspects I'm one. Right?'

'Right,' he agreed, his lips tilting up at one corner in sardonic appreciation of her forthright-ness. 'Are you?' he challenged her.

'I couldn't marry only for money,' she replied.

'Then what would you marry for?' he asked.

'Love,' she said honestly, and he laughed, his eyes dancing suddenly with merriment, his white teeth flashing, his lean face creasing attractively.

'You English, always so romantic,' he mocked.

'You don't believe me?' Marina retorted as she picked up her knife and fork.

'I don't believe people should marry for romantic love only,' he replied. 'It would be foolish to marry someone with whom one had had perhaps one romantic episode.' He also picked up his knife and fork and began to cut his meat. After a while Marina asked,

'Does Giovanni Barberini live on Biscari?'

'He does.'

'And does he know Frankie has invited me to go and stay there for a while?'

'My sister has informed him, so if you accept the invitation you can be sure that everything you do and say will be watched and listened to and reported back to Grandfather Barberini,' he said dryly.

'Then I'm surprised Frankie has been allowed to invite me, considering how much his grandfather and his mother were against his friendship with me over a year ago,' she remarked.

'Lucia is a very loving mother. Francesco is her only child and she dotes on him, so will do anything he asks. She seems to think that when he sees you again a miracle will happen and he'll be able to walk again. Giovanni also cares very much for Francesco, and that is why he has agreed to let you stay on Biscari.' Vittorio Matissi looked up and gave her a sardonic glance. 'Of course, if Giovanni finds you unacceptable as a companion for his grandson you will be asked to leave.'

'And if I refuse to leave? What then?'

'You'll be removed.'

'Mafia tactics?' she challenged him with a lightness she wasn't feeling. The thought of having everything she did and said reported back to Frankie's grandfather chilled her.

'You can describe Giovanni's methods in that way if you wish,' he replied with a shrug. 'but I doubt if you really know what you mean when you use the word *mafia*.'

'I know that there's an organisation which uses illegal methods such as threats of murder and blackmail to get what it wants for its members which is called the Mafia and that it started in Sicily,' she retorted.

'You are talking about the American organisation,' he replied equably. 'And it is true there is a group over there known as the Mafia which uses illegal methods. It is true also that Mafia with a capital *M* started in Sicily. It is a sort of private army developed from the small armies of the feudal times when Norman overlords imposed their rule on Sicily. But that organisation doesn't exist in the eastern part of Sicily and its threats are terrifying only in Palermo or Partinico. They are ignored in Catania where I come from, and neither the Barberini family nor the Matissi family are associated with the Mafia.' He paused and sipped more wine. 'But on the other hand,' he went on, 'all Sicilians possess *mafia* spelt with a small *m*.

And that is a state of mind, a moral code which we all share. It is taught from the cradle, and we grow up knowing we should always help our families in time of need, fight common enemies and side with our families even if the enemy is right and the family is wrong. Do you understand?'

'I think so. It's a sort of clannishness, like Highland Scots have.'

'*Si*, that is close to it. So you see in wanting to protect his grandson, who is also the heir to his considerable fortune, Giovanni Barberini is being *mafioso* in that sense.'

'But what about Frankie? Isn't he allowed to choose whom he likes to be his companion or his wife?' she exclaimed. She was so accustomed to freedom of choice herself that she was thoroughly revolted by the idea of having to choose to please family pride.

'Only in so far as he chooses a woman who is compatible with his way of life and his family.' He paused, his mouth twisting slightly. 'It seems he has chosen you and nothing anyone has said to him will change his mind, so you've been invited to Biscari to be looked over and evaluated to find out if you are suitable. How does that appeal to you?'

'It doesn't,' Marina replied with a little shudder.

'Does that mean you're going to refuse the invitation?' he asked softly.

Marina laid down her knife and fork and picked up her wine-glass. Over the glass she studied Vittorio Matissi's face, sensing a subtle change in his attitude. The expression in his dark eyes was frankly sensual now as they appraised her face. He was looking at her as he might look at any woman whose physical appearance pleased him. He was looking at her as if he would like to spend a few hours making love to her. The message came through to her clearly, shocking her yet exciting her too. Her eyelashes fluttered down defensively, and she sipped quickly at the wine, amazed at the reaction of her own senses to the way he was looking at her. Deep down inside her she felt something uncoiling itself, an overpowering aching urge to go away with him to a quiet and private place where they could be alone together and explore each other's bodies and minds.

Her hand shook, wine slopped from the glass on to the tablecloth. She set the glass down quickly and said as coolly as she could,

'Do you want me to refuse it?'

In a strange silence they stared at each other. The moment came to an abrupt end when a waiter came to the table to remove their plates. Vittorio Matissi sat back in his chair, the expression in his eyes hidden by their heavy lids.

'What I want has nothing to do with this,' he said coolly. 'I'm merely the go-between, a messenger from Frankie and his mother.'

For some reason Marina felt as if he had just reached out and pushed her away from him. The feeling was strange. A waiter came and filled up their wine glasses with more red wine and took their order for dessert and coffee.

'I'd like to know more about Biscari, please,' she said, retreating to her former position, wishing she had never tried to get closer to him by asking him if he wanted her to refuse the invitation.

'Like many of the small islands scattered around the Italian and Sicilian coastline, it is volcanic in origin,' he replied rather stiltedly, not looking at her. 'There are olive groves, tiny yellow beaches, pinewoods, high cliffs and rocky caves. There are also the remains of ancient Greek temples and Roman villas as well as some Byzantine and Baroque churches. Giovanni lives in the old *castello*, which is of Moorish design. The house where Frankie lives with his mother is like an up-to-date Roman villa and quite luxurious. The weather is much better than it is here.' He grimaced at the window. The rain seemed to have increased in its intensity. 'If you decide to accept my sister will make you very welcome,' he added indifferently.

There was nothing persuasive in his manner. He was merely reciting facts, and again Marina felt quite strongly that he didn't want her to accept Frankie's invitation, that he would think even less of her than he did already if she did accept. She glanced at him from under her lashes. He had finished his wine and was staring into his empty glass.

'I . . . I'd like to go and see Frankie very much,' she said at last. 'But I can't go right away.'

'Why not?' He looked up sharply. 'The woman at the agency told me you're not working at the moment and so you are free to travel.'

'I haven't worked since the accident. It . . . it took a long time for me to recover and to learn to walk again. I've used up all my savings, so I can't afford to go to Biscari right now. I'll ... I'll have to find a job and save up.'

Vittorio Matissi folded his arms on the table and leaned forward, his glance flicking over her face searchingly as if he were trying to find the answer to a puzzle.

'If you accept the invitation your first class air fare will be paid for,' he told her. 'All your expenses will be paid. That is the offer I have been instructed to make to you. So, do you accept the invitation?'

There was another silence between them. All around them were the hum of voices and the soft sounds of waiters moving about. There was nothing warm or sensual in the way Vittorio Matissi was looking at her now, she thought, nothing of the lover of women in his manner. His square-jawed face was set in hard lines, his broad-lipped mouth was closed in a straight unsmiling line and his dark eyes were narrowed to slits. The impression she had that he was hoping she would refuse to accept Frankie's invitation puzzled her. Why didn't he want her to accept? The only reason she could find to explain his antipathy towards herself was that he didn't think she was good enough for Frankie.

Yes, that must be why. He had shown already that he didn't approve of her past association with his nephew, and now he wasn't prepared to encourage her future association with Frankie. That touched her pride in herself. Immediately she wanted to show him she was good enough to be the companion or wife of Frankie no matter how wealthy he was.

'I accept,' she said quietly. 'I'd like to go and visit Frankie very much.'

'I thought you might,' he murmured, with that mocking twist to his mouth. 'Once you heard all expenses would bc paid.'

Marina's fingers tightened around the stem of her wine glass.

'You were hoping I'd refuse the invitation, weren't you?' she challenged.

'Was I? Whatever makes you think that?' he retorted mockingly, taking a small notebook from a pocket and opening it. 'Would you please give me your address here in London, and also your telephone number, if you have one, so that I can contact you when I've made the arrangements for you to travel to Biscari?'

She gave him the address and watched him write it down, still feeling angry with him for some reason.

'You think I've accepted only because I'll get something for nothing, a free Mediterranean holiday, don't you?' she accused him furiously.

'And haven't you?'

'No, I haven't. Oh, I don't expect you to understand this, but I've accepted the invitation because I like Frankie—really like him for himself, and not because he's heir to a fortune. And I'm sorry he can't walk. I know what it's like to be in his position and be afraid I might never walk again—I've been there quite recently. So I want to go and help him, to offer my sympathy and encouragement. I want to help him.'

'You're right. I don't understand such romantic altruism,' Vittorio Matissi replied cynically. 'In my experience few people do anything outside their own family unless they're hoping for some sort of payment in return.'

'Oh, you are. . . .' She broke off, speechless with a strange impotent anger because his attitude was so different from her own.

'A realist,' he supplied with a slight grin. 'I don't believe in your romantic idealism and I don't practise it. I think you use it as a cover to hide your real aim in life, and right now you're out of work, you have no marriage prospects in sight, so it suits you very well to go and see Frankie, all expenses paid, in the hope that you'll be accepted by his family and will become his wife.'

Something happened to Marina then. There was a roaring in her ears and his dark mocking face, the darkness of his eyes blurred before her eyes. She lifted her wine-glass and threw the remains of her wine across the table at his face. Red drops appeared on his chin and mouth. Crimson stained the collar of his white shirt.

Menace glared at her from the depths of his eyes, but he didn't move. With an exclamation of distress because she had allowed him to provoke her into behaving badly Marina sprang to her feet. The chair tipped over backwards behind her. Aware that the people at the next table were staring at her and that waiters were advancing from all directions, she ran from the room.

Down the long hallway with its elegant alcoves she rushed headlong, hardly noticing the steps down to the foyer. In the cloakroom she handed over the ticket for her coat. Once she had the coat on she paused to arrange the hat on her head and leaning towards the mirror outlined her lips with fresh lipstick. Then she hurried out into the foyer and towards the revolving doors.

Outside she hesitated as cold air made her catch her breath. A hand gripped her elbow and she swung round. Vittorio Matissi smiled down at her. It was a smile without mirth, white-toothed, glacial. His dark eyes were still shooting red sparks at her.

'This way. The taxi has come,' he said pleasantly.

Helpless in the steel-like grip of his hand, Marina was forced to walk across the wet pavement and to step into the waiting cab.

CHAPTER TWO

THE door of the taxi slammed shut and Vittorio Matissi sat down beside her. The taxi moved out into the traffic. Marina felt again the weight of Vittorio's shoulder against hers and the sinewy muscularity of his thigh against hers and she moved, sliding along the seat until she was close to the outside door. Her head averted from him, she stared out at the cars and buses, at the people hurrying along pavements, umbrellas bobbing. Lights shone from shop windows as if it were evening instead of half-past one in the middle of the day.

The taxi turned into Piccadilly and drove towards the Circus. From there it made slow progress to the Mall and began to go towards Buckingham Palace.

'Where are we going?' Marina demanded.

'I've told the driver to drive around anywhere he likes. We'll drive around until you apologise for throwing wine in my face.' Anger throbbed in the deep voice. 'It isn't often I lose my temper, but *Dio mio*, you would provoke a saint, and that's something I've never been nor hoped to be!'

'It isn't often I lose my temper either,' Marina retorted. 'But I don't see why I should apologise to you. In fact I'm not going to apologise until you take back the insults you handed out to me in the restaurant.'

'Then we shall be driving around for a long time,' he said through his teeth.

She turned her head to look at him. The white trenchcoat he had slung over his suit to protect it from the sleet emphasised his darkness, Mephistopheles, the devil's messenger, in a raincoat sitting in the back of a London taxi, she thought fancifully. Only he wasn't the devil's messenger. He was Francesco's messenger, and he was very angry, his lean face taut, the finely chiselled nostrils of his nose flaring, his even white teeth gritted together, one hand clenched on his knee.

'An Englishman would have laughed at what I did,' Marina said tauntingly.

'But I am not an Englishman,' he retorted, flicking her a glittering hostile glance. 'And no one, not even a woman, gets away with insulting me in a public place the way you did.'

'You insulted me, so I retaliated in the only way I could think of. I had warned you,' she flung at him. 'You have no right to make assumptions about me just because I've earned my living as a fashion model! You're arrogant and prejudiced, and I'm not going to apologise for showing you what I think of your opinion of me.'

She leaned forward, intending to knock on the glass partition so as to get the attention of the cab driver to ask him to stop, but before her hand had touched the partition she was seized roughly from behind and flung against the back of the seat.

'Take your hands off me!' she snapped, glaring up at the dark face poised above hers, and her fingers curved to claw at him. Vittorio Matissi caught her hand in his. She opened her mouth to shout, but swiftly he bent his head and his lips pressed hard against hers, smothering her cry, reducing it to a muffled explosion of sound.

The weight of his chest and shoulders pinned her against the back of the seat. One hand trapped in his, the other trapped between their two bodies, she couldn't move. Her neck was beginning to ache and panic was beginning to rise in her when suddenly his lips began to move against hers slowly and seductively, coaxing hers to respond. He let go of her hand so he could stroke the hair back from her temple. Taking advantage of the change in him, she managed to slide her mouth from beneath his. She opened her lips to shout again and once again they were covered by his.

A long time passed before he lifted his mouth from hers; endless moments during which a kiss intended to silence her developed into a kiss of seduction, drawing from her a deeply primitive response, until the hungry desire which was in her met and answered the hungry desire which was in him. And when it was over she found she was shaking not with anger nor with fear but with passion which had flared up so unexpectedly in reply to his sense-inflaming caress.

But she wasn't going to let him know how much she had been affected by his kiss. Wiping the back of her hand across her throbbing lips, she glared at him.

'I could sue you for assault!' she hissed.

He gave her a scornful look from beneath his lashes and moved away to tap on the glass partition. Leaning forward, he instructed the driver to go to the address where Marina lived.

The taxi turned in the middle of a street along which it had been cruising and began to go back the way it had come. Relieved because Vittorio seemed to have realised the futility of driving around the West End while he waited for her to apologise, Marina opened her handbag, took out her compact and inspected her face in the small mirror. Her cheeks were flushed, there was a small dark bruise on her lip and her blue-grey eyes were glittering with a strange wild light.

Not liking what she saw, she snapped the compact closed and returned it to her handbag. She pulled the skirt of her suit straight—it had ridden up above her knees to expose her rounded limbs—and wrapped her fur coat about her. Sitting straight in her corner, she slanted a glance sideways at Vittorio Matissi.

His legs were stretched out before him, and his head was tilted back against the back of the seat. His hands were thrust into his trouser pockets and he was staring straight ahead, the frown, which had brought his thick eyebrows together, grimly forbidding. His lips were compressed into a tight thin line.

As if he had become aware of her gaze he turned his head and looked at her. They stared at each other as if they were seeing each other for the first time. Time passed in silence as the taxi lurched along streets, turned corners, stopped and started at traffic lights.

'I was wrong,' Vittorio spoke abruptly, his glance never wavering, his eyes transmitting messages to her that were quite different from his words. 'I shouldn't have made assumptions about you, and I shouldn't have said what I did,' he added. 'I apologise for that.'

'Thank you,' she said primly, and looked away out of the window. They were in Chelsea now, not far from where she lived.

'But I'm not going to apologise for kissing you. I'm glad I kissed you, so you can go ahead and sue me for assault if you want,' he continued harshly. 'I have no defence. You provoked me in a way no woman has ever done before.'

Still staring out of the window, Marina bit her lip. Now she was wishing her meeting with him could have been otherwise. She wished she could have met him before the car accident, before she had become involved with Francesco, even before she had met Steve. She wished he had been the first man she had ever known, her first love. She wished they had met before her face had become known internationally on the cover of a fashion magazine.

'I'm sorry too,' she whispered. 'I'm sorry it couldn't have been different. . . .' She paused, biting her lip again, not knowing how to express her confusion, not sure whether she should. She turned towards him. 'I'm sorry I threw the wine at you,' she went on more coolly. 'I hope your shirt isn't stained forever.' She looked down at her hands. 'I've never done anything like that in my life before. I don't know what came over me,' she added, whispering again and shaking her head from side to side.

'Friction,' he said, and she looked at him again. He was still looking at her, but the grimness had faded from his face. 'Static electricity. We strike sparks from each other and possibly it would have been safer for both of us if we had never met.' He shrugged fatalistically. 'But we have met, and what will be will be,' he added as the taxi swerved in towards a kerb. He looked out of the window beside him. 'This is where you live?'

'Yes.'

'Alone?'

'No. I'm staying with a friend of mine, sharing her flat.'

'Don't you have a family?'

'Of course, but my parents are out of the country, working in Nigeria for the British Trade Commission,' she replied coolly.

'I still don't have a telephone number,' he said.

She gave it to him and he wrote it down.

'I'll need a day or two to get ready. I can't leave until Thursday at the latest,' she said.

'So I will make reservations for you to fly on Thursday. I leave London myself tomorrow, but I'll be at the Catania airport to meet you and I'll take you over to Biscari. I'll phone you this evening about seven with the information about the flight.'

'Thank you,' she said stiffly.

He opened the door beside him and stepped out on to the pavement to hold the door open while she stepped out of the cab.

'*Arrivederci,*' he said briskly, and before Marina had a chance to reply he got back into the taxi. The door slammed shut and the vehicle moved away.

She was in her bedroom sorting through her clothes, trying to decide which to take with her, when her friend Annis called her to the phone. Vittorio Matissi wasted no time in pleasantries but went straight to the point, giving her the times of departure and arrival of the flight to Catania, then told her where she could pick up the ticket. He said again he would be at Catania airport to meet her on Thursday afternoon and rang off. Marina put the receiver back slowly on its rest. He had made it quite clear that he wished to have as little to do with her as possible, and perhaps he had been right when he had said it would have been safer for both of them if they had never met.

Three days later when the big jet soared into the air she felt a sense of having escaped at last from a prison. For that was what the car crash had done to her. It had imprisoned her for nearly fifteen months, making it impossible for her to do her work, which had involved much travel. Sitting at her ease in the first class section of the plane, she thought how wonderful it would be to fly forever in that world above the clouds, where the sky was perpetually blue and the sun was always shining, to travel in space far beyond the problems associated with living on earth.

The hours of escape passed all too quickly. She slept a little. She ate a meal. She stared and stared out of the window. *What is this life if, full of care, we have no time to stand and stare?* The lines from W. H. Davies' poem went round and round in her head.

Too soon the plane began to lose height to begin its descent towards the land. A cone-shaped mountain tilting skywards appeared. Smoke seemed to be coming out of a huge crater. The rock was charcoal grey, barren, runnelled with winter snow. Lower down, the slopes were scarred with patches of yellow. It was Mount Etna, Europe's biggest and most active volcano, the smiling Italian stewardess informed Marina when she asked about it. In its time it had destroyed the city of Catania. It awed and humbled and inspired a respect (or was it fear?) of the natural phenomena of the earth.

Half an hour later Marina stood in the arrivals lounge at the airport terminal building surrounded by chattering and exclaiming Sicilian families who had come to meet relatives or friends arriving from overseas. She looked around, searching for Vittorio Matissi. He wasn't there, and she stood waiting for him in the same place, afraid to move away in case she missed him, for about twenty minutes.

At last he came, striding right up to her to take hold of her shoulders and to kiss her briefly on both cheeks, much to her surprise, just as if she was a member of his family.

'Couldn't you have been here on time?' she complained crossly. 'I've just spent the most uncomfortable twenty minutes of my life being stared at, ogled and even importuned by some of your countrymen!'

His dark glance flashed over her appearance and came back to her face.

'I'm not surprised,' he remarked. 'You should have worn something less eye-catching.'

'This is eye-catching?' She looked down at her culotte suit which was made from burgundy-coloured wool.

'Compared with what most Sicilian women wear, it is. It draws attention to you by its strangeness, and by wearing it here you're more or less asking to have a pass made at you. A Sicilian woman would never travel in such an outfit.'

'I am not a Sicilian woman,' she retorted haughtily.

'I had noticed,' he mocked, his lips twitching into a grin as his glance lingered admiringly on her blonde hair which she was wearing loosely, curving in rough casual waves from a centre parting down to her shoulders. 'Is this all your luggage?' He picked up her two suitcases.

His car was of Italian make, small, sporty and fast, and he drove it as if the police were chasing him. Glad of the seat belt, Marina clung to the handle on the inside of the door as they careered along a narrow roadway towards the city. Unable to stand the sight of everything rocketing towards her and then past her at great speed, she closed her eyes. It was a mistake. At once she was in another car, sitting beside another man in the darkness, hurtling through grey fog along a winding English road. She was with Francesco and he was driving too fast.

'Please, oh, please, won't you drive more slowly!' she gasped. 'We're going to crash if you don't, we're going to crash!'

The car slowed down, stopped. Marina opened her eyes and turned to Vittorio. An arm resting on the steering wheel, he had turned to her.

'I am sorry,' he said. 'I had forgotten you had been hurt in that accident. But I would have thought that by now you'd have got your nerve back.'

'I thought I had, too,' she whispered. 'It was just that . . . oh, do you have to drive so fast?'

'If we wish to catch the ferryboat to Biscari today, yes, I do have to drive fast. You see, I was late meeting you because of a business meeting which went on too long, so now I am late going for the ferry. It goes only once a day at this time of the year. If we miss it you will have to stay the night in Catania, and Francesco will be disappointed when you don't arrive this afternoon.' He paused, his glance going to her hands which were twisting nervously together on her lap. His hand reached out and covered hers, grasping them firmly.

'Where would I stay if we miss the ferry?' she muttered, staring down at the olive-skinned, black-flecked hand.

'At my house,' he replied. 'Outside Catania. I think it would be wiser for us to catch the ferry, don't you?'

She gave him a startled upward glance from under her lashes. He was leaning towards her and for a moment she was mesmerised by the expression in his heavy-lidded brown eyes. Then it occurred to her that he was looking at her in the same way that the men at the airport had looked at her, and it was in his blood and bones to make a pass at an attractive woman in the same way it was in their blood and bones. She withdrew her hands hastily from his and looked away out of the car window.

'Yes, I do think it would be wiser for us to catch the ferry,' she said stiffly. 'I don't want to disappoint Frankie.'

'Then try to relax and remember we are here and not in England on a foggy night and I'm not Frankie. I'm sober and I can see where I'm going. There will be no accident,' he assured her.

He released the brake, his foot went down on the clutch, his hand brushed her thigh as it reached out to the gear lever and, with a screech of tyres on the loose gravel of the shoulder of the road they were off again, surging towards the city of Catania which glinted in the spring sunlight against the blue sky.

It was better not to look at the surface of the road hurtling towards her, thought Matrina. But where could she look? Only at Vittorio Matissi. Dressed in a cream turtlenecked sweater under a jacket of fine grey tweed, he seemed a very different person from the suave businessman she had met in London. He was younger-looking, more handsome than she had remembered, less the severe disapproving uncle of Frankie.

He must have been only fifteen when Frankie, who was now twenty and two years younger than herself, had been born. She thought of her own uncles. Her mother's brother, David, was about fifty, bald, paunchy and good-natured, a father and a grandfather. Her father's brother, Michael, a professor of physics, was tall and thin, his grey hair was always in a tangle, and he was also a father and about to become a grandfather.

But Vittorio Matissi wasn't even married. Why? Wasn't it unusual for a Sicilian man of his age to be unmarried? Marina felt a sudden burning curiosity about him. She wanted to know all about him. No, she mustn't be tempted to try to get closer to him. They would only strike sparks off each other.

'You know about Catania?' he asked abruptly.

'Only that it was once destroyed by an eruption from Mount Etna,' she replied. The car was going more slowly now, weaving in and out of the traffic on a main thoroughfare in the city.

'It has been destroyed more than once by Etna and also by earthquakes and invading armies,' he told her. 'But each time it was rebuilt, and the main street is called Via Etnea.' A crease appeared in his cheek as he grinned. 'It takes a certain amount of bravado for a town to name its main street after the volcano which had destroyed it. But that's Catania—bold, optimistic, energetic.'

Marina looked out again. The city seemed to be planned in a series of straight streets and right angles and was embellished with sumptuous Baroque churches. Many of the buildings had been constructed from the same cooled grey lava as the distant towering mountain. In a square a lava-grey elephant stood in the centre under the spray of a fountain and a huge cathedral, built mostly in Baroque style, with a dome, a belfry, a balustrade decorated with sculptured figures and Roman columns enhancing its façade, sprawled along one side of the square.

A brisk wind whipped the blue waters of the harbour and made flags snap at the top of their poles. Vittorio parked his car among a crowd of other cars, and carrying Marina's two suitcases, he hurried towards the wharf where the ferryboat was tied up. Its white paint sleek, its stainless steel fittings glittering, it resembled a motor yacht, and the name *Biscari* was painted in red on its stern. Hardly had they stepped aboard than the gangway was drawn up and the lines were cast off. With a deep throb of its engines the boat swung away from the wharf. Gathering speed, it swooshed across the dancing wind-tossed waves and out to sea.

After seeing that she was seated by a window in the pleasant saloon Vittorio disappeared. For a while Marina sat watching the water sliding by. There were a few people in the saloon besides herself, all of them women; all of them dressed in black, all of them staring at her. She assumed they were islanders who had been to the mainland to shop, judging by their many parcels and shopping bags.

When it dawned on her that Vittorio was not coming back to the saloon Marina grew restless. He had left her in this place, presumably where women always sat, out of the wind and out of the way of their menfolk. Well, she wasn't going to stay there, unable to see where the boat was going. She stood up and began to walk towards one of the sliding doors that opened on to the side-deck. The boat was rolling from side to side and she approached the door in a little rush. She slid the door open and stepped outside.

Immediately her hair was whipped back from her face and the thin woollen culotte suit was flattened against the contours of her body. Staggering a little as the deck swayed beneath her feet, she pushed against the wind towards the bow of the boat. As she had expected, some passengers, all men, were standing on the foredeck leaning against the rails, watching the bow wave curl against the forefoot of the ship. Vittorio was the farthest away and was alone. Marina pushed her way to his side and leaned her arms on the rail too.

'Is the island in sight yet?' She had to raise her voice above the throb of engines, the swish of water and the whistle of the wind.

'Over there.' He pointed and she saw a greyish-green hump in the distance. 'Why have you come up here?'

'I didn't like being in the saloon with all those women staring at my clothes,' she confessed. She turned to look at him and her hair was whipped into a tangle about her face. 'I think it was very bad-mannered of you not to ask me if I would like to come up here,' she said challengingly.

'Most women don't like being blown about.' He shrugged his shoulders indifferently.

'Another of your arrogant male assumptions,' she retorted. Now her hair was streaming sideways and blowing right across his face. She caught hold of the errant blonde strands and held them down to her head. 'I've been sailing most of my life and I've been to sea many times on my father's small boat.'

He turned sideways to the rail to look at her properly. His own windblown hair was standing out from his head like a halo of curling black feathers.

'If I'd known you can sail and like sailing I'd have taken you to Biscari on *Nesaea*,' he said.

'*Nesaea?*'

'My yacht.' He jerked his head in the direction

of Catania. 'It's in the harbour, thirty-five feet overall, ketch-rigged and built in England. I bought it because the price was low and because the name appealed to me. *Nesaea* was a sea-nymph, a Nereid, one of the daughters of Nereus, the Old Man of the Sea in mythology, and I felt a boat named for her should be here, in the Mediterranean. We've visited many islands, *Nesaea* and I.'

He spoke quietly and with conviction, and Marina sensed immediately that his love of the sea was like her own, not a stormy obsession, an infatuation for someone he did not see clearly and didn't know well, but a durable feeling, one that went right back to his childhood and would last as long as he lived. It surprised her and cracked the wall of prejudice she had built up to protect herself against him.

'I wish too that you had known I can sail and like sailing,' she murmured. 'I would have loved to have gone to Biscari on your yacht.'

They stood looking at each other. It was another of those dangerous moments like the one in the taxi in London after Vittorio had kissed her; like the one in his car on the way from the airport to Catania. The veils which had hidden them from each other were gradually being lifted. In time they would see each other much more clearly, would know each other better, and then. . . .

Vittorio moved fast, turning away to lean his arms on the top of the rail and to look out at the island which was growing higher as the ship approached it. Details were appearing; the squares and rectangles of flat-roofed houses climbing grey-green hillsides; the dome of a church glittering in the sunlight; and on top of a cliff, which rose straight up out of the splashing sea, an ancient building, a sort of castle with a row of battlements and many Moorish arches.

'No, it's safer for us to come to Biscari this way,' Vittorio murmured mysteriously. 'We will arrive on time and Francesco won't be disappointed.'

It was silly to feel as if she had been rejected. After all, she hadn't really expected anything from him. Yet a feeling of sadness flooded through her as she stared out at the island and once again she found herself wishing she could have met him in different circumstances.

The boat berthed in the small harbour, which was protected by a sea wall built of rough stone which glowed pink in the sunlight. Brightly coloured fishing boats and some small pleasure craft bobbed up and down on the wash created by the incoming ferry. Houses, glowing pink and white in the sunlight, crowded close to the narrow wharf, as if being pushed into the sea by the cliffs behind them.

Once they were ashore Vittorio led the way to a long black car which was waiting on the wharf. It was driven by a squat, wide-shouldered man with a sallow face and sleek black hair who looked as if he should have been a fisherman rather than a chauffeur. Leaving the wharf, the car nosed up a narrow street past old houses. Most had tiny balconies outside long windows edged with

shutters. Washing hung over the rails of the
balconies to dry. Women clustered in doorways
talking. Children played ball in the middle of the
street, running to the sides when they heard the car
approaching.

Soon the fishing village was left behind. The
road climbed upwards, higher and higher through
a grove of carefully tended olive trees. On the
other side of the grove the road ended in front of a
sprawling white villa built on a cliffside above a
small bay of limpid blue-green water protected
from the swell of the sea by two rocky
promontories covered with pinewoods. In a corner
of the bay, a small motor cruiser swung at a
mooring.

From the car Vittorio led the way up some wide
steps on to a loggia, a gallery which projected
from one side of the building and was open to the
air. Its roof was supported by stone pillars around
which leafy vines twined. Vittorio pushed open one
side of the double door and Marina stepped past
him into a wide entrance hall. The floor was a
mosaic of blue-green and white tiles. White pillars
supported an upper gallery. Behind them doors
opened into rooms. The centre of the hall was
comfortably furnished with long Roman-style
sofas and long low coffee tables. Two women were
sitting on one of the sofas talking. They looked
round on hearing Vittorio and Marina's footsteps
and both stood up. The elder of the two, a broad-
shouldered, ample-bosomed woman with thick
curling black hair plentifully sprinkled with grey,
came forward, her hands outstretched in greeting

to Vittorio. He embraced her, then turned to Marina.

'I forgot to ask you if you can speak Italian,' he murmured. 'This is my eldest sister, Lucia. She has very little English.'

'I have a few phrases,' Marina said coolly, and held out her hand to Lucia Barberini, who was staring at the burgundy outfit, her black eyes wide and incredulous. Marina smiled her most brilliant smile.

'*Buon giorno, signora. Io sono* Marina Gregson,' she said.

'*Buon giorno, signorina. Comè sta?*' Lucia smiled hesitantly, then added in heavily accented English, 'You are very welcome.' She lost her nervousness suddenly and laughed, a warm chuckle of sound. '*Mi scusi, signorina.* I do not speak *Inglese* well.' She went off into a spate of Italian, her plump beringed hands moving all the time, her dark eyes flashing. Then she ended by saying, to Vittorio, 'Tell her,' she pointed at Marina, 'tell her what I say.'

'Did you grasp anything of what she said?' Vittorio asked with a sigh.

'No, I'm afraid not.'

'She said you are more beautiful than the photographs she has seen of you, more beautiful than Francesco says you are. You are like an angel come from heaven.' He paused, then said in a stage whisper, 'Lucia always did have a tendency to exaggerate, so don't let anything she says go to your head.'

Marina flashed him a scornful glance, but he

had turned away and was going forward to greet
the other woman, who had remained standing
beside the sofa. She was younger than Lucia,
possibly a little younger than Vittorio, and was tall
with a beautifully-proportioned figure, draped in a
silky dress which Marina guessed had been
designed by Marius, the Paris designer she herself
had modelled for. The woman embraced Vittorio,
kissing him on the cheek affectionately, then made
some smiling remarks to him.

'Marina, this is Frankie's aunt, his father's
younger sister, Emilia Rossi, who has just arrived
from the United States,' said Vittorio, and the
woman moved towards Marina with her hand held
out.

'I am also pleased to meet you, Miss Gregson,'
Emilia said crisply and clearly. 'I've also admired
photographs of you and I've even seen you
modelling at one of Marius's shows in New
York.' Perfectly moulded lips curved back from
perfect almond-shaped teeth. Dark grey eyes
glinted between mascaraed lashes. 'We missed you
at last year's show. Will you be modelling for
Marius again, later this year?'

'I'm not sure,' replied Marina. There was
something patronising about the elegant woman
that irritated her. She felt herself recoiling
inwardly while outwardly she continued to smile
seraphically. On her right Lucia spoke again and
Vittorio translated.

'Lucia says she will show you to your room. She
says you will probably want to freshen up after the
journey and to change your clothes before seeing

Francesco. At the moment he is with his physiotherapist doing exercises. My sister suggests you should change into a dress.' Mockery rippled through the deep musical voice. 'She assumes you have a suitable one with you.'

Their eyes met across the space that separated them. It was a brief meeting of minds, a sharing of amusement, and was over quickly when Emilia Rossi intervened, slipping her hand into the crook of Vittorio's arm and turning him away to whisper something to him before they walked away together under the gallery and through an open doorway into another room.

The room Marina was shown to by her hostess was light and airy painted in pale colours and furnished with thick-piled carpeting, white-painted chests and dressing table and a wide bed, with a frilled canopy and a flounced, quilted silken bedcover. Frilly net curtains stirred in the sea-breeze that wafted in through the slightly open long windows. From the windows there was a magnificent view of the small horseshoe-shaped bay, the headlands protecting it and beyond the blue, blue sea shimmering with scales of silver under the equally blue sunlit sky.

Soothed by the comfort and tasteful furnishings of the room, Marina unpacked her clothes and hung them in the closet. In the sea-green bathroom she washed, then returned to the bedroom to choose a dress. Remembering the elegance of Emilia Rossi she chose the most expensive dress she had with her. Made from blue silk it was subtly simple, a plain skirt belted at the waist, long

sleeves ending in ruffles at the wrists. Only the
bodice was unusual and attention-drawing. The
neckline was a deep plunging V that exposed the
cleft between her bare breasts and one side of the
V was decorated by a long frill matching the
ruffles at her wrists.

She was just making up her face when there was
a knock on the door. She called out,

'Come in,' then remembered belatedly she was on
a Sicilian island, and went over to the door to
open it. Before she reached it it opened slowly and
Emilia Rossi entered the room.

'Lucia asked me to come and see if you're ready
to meet Francesco,' Emilia said, closing the door
behind her. Her eyes considered the blue silk dress
and she raised one long-fingered hand, glittering
with diamonds and sapphires, to press fingertips
against a golden-skinned cheek in a gesture of
dismay. 'Oh, *Dio mio*, that dress! Isn't it just a
little too much for the occasion?' she said softly.
'We're only going to have tea on the loggia, a
friendly family occasion. You and Francesco
won't be alone. There won't be any time for
romance.'

She doesn't like me, thought Marina. We've
only just met and already she doesn't like me and
she's determined to put me in my place. Why?
What have I ever done to her?

'Then what do you suggest I should wear?' she
asked coolly. Stepping over to the clothes closet,
she pushed back the sliding door. 'Come and help
me to decide,' she suggested.

Emilia took her at her word and examined the

clothes seriously, choosing at last a knife-pleated skirt of grey wool and a long-sleeved blouse with a high frilled neckline made from dark green silk. They were clothes that certainly covered up, thought Marina wryly, as she slipped them on. They made her look demure but older than she was. They subdued her.

'That is much better,' said Emilia with a smile. She examined her own appearance in the long mirror and seemed satisfied with what she saw. 'A word of advice—if you wish to make an impression on my father appear to be submissive and decorous at all times, even if you are not really like that. He does not like overbearing, domineering, liberated women.'

'Why would I want to make an impression on your father?' Marina asked.

'Isn't that why you've been invited here?' Emilia exclaimed. 'Lucia has told me everything, you know. How Francesco is crazy about you and wants to marry you. But he won't be allowed to marry you unless my father approves of you. So if you really want to be accepted, if you really want to marry Francesco, you'll do your best to please his grandfather. Are you ready to come and see Francesco now?'

'Yes, I'm ready.'

'How long have you been travelling today?' Emilia asked politely as they left the room to walk along the passage to the entrance hall.

'I left London this morning,' said Marina.

'With Vittorio?' queried Emilia.

'No. He met me at Catania airport.'

'But you and he have met before?'

'Yes, a few days ago in London.'

'Vittorio and I are very good friends,' Emilia went on chattily. 'We go back a long way to the time when Lucia married my brother Guido. Later Vittorio and I wanted to marry each other, but it wasn't possible.' She sighed heavily.

'Oh, why?' asked Marina.

'Vittorio's father died suddenly and it was discovered that the Matissi company was bankrupt, and Vittorio had to turn all his attention to building the business up again. He was too poor to marry me. So Father arranged my marriage to Eugenio Rossi, an Italian-American millionaire, instead. He was pleased with the connection.' Emilia's voice grated rather bitterly.

'But I thought—well, I had the impression that Mr Matissi is successful and wealthy too,' said Marina as they entered the entrance hall.

'He is now, fourteen years too late,' said Emilia caustically.

They crossed the hall to the front door without saying anything else. Emilia opened the door and held it back, but Marina hesitated, suddenly reluctant to meet Frankie again while members of his family were present.

'Such enthusiasm,' Emilia remarked dryly, raising a scornful eyebrow. 'Not that I blame you. There have been some drastic changes made to Francesco's appearance since that accident. All right, I'll go first.'

She stepped outside, her high heels clicking on the tiles. Marina wetted her lips, pushed her hair back from her face, straightened her shoulders and stepped through the door, her head up, her lips smiling.

Although aware of Lucia and Vittorio sitting on wooden garden chairs she saw only the wheelchair, placed so that Frankie could see the front door, and she went straight to him to put her hands in his outstretched ones. She looked down into dark grey eyes which were raised imploringly to hers and felt shock quiver through her when she saw the white mask plastic surgery had made of one side of his face. Something broke within her and compassion came flooding out.

'Oh, my dear, how good it is to see you!' she whispered, and going down on her knees beside him she put her arms around him and kissed him on both cheeks.

CHAPTER THREE

THE sun was setting. In the west the sky was crimson streaked with golden clouds. The sea was also crimson, but changing swiftly as dusk approached to that wine-dark colour first described by Homer. The stone pillars of the loggia gleamed with a ghostly light and the air was scented with pines and olive trees. From somewhere lower down the hillside came the sound of music; strange music played on a reed instrument, its rhythm swaying and sensuous, its sound thin and plaintive; music that was more Arabian than European.

Marina sat on a cushioned stool close to Frankie. Her arm rested on his knee and her hand was clasped in his. They were alone. Lucia had gone into the house on the pretext of talking to the cook about dinner and Emilia had persuaded Vittorio to go walking in the garden with her.

'They know I want to talk to you privately,' Francesco whispered. 'I can hardly believe you're here.'

'And I feel as if I'm dreaming,' she replied with a laugh. 'This place has a dreamlike quality. It's so beautiful, so peaceful. I hope I don't wake up soon and find myself in London, hurrying to catch the bus, running through the puddles and the rain!'

'You won't,' he assured her. 'You're here, on Biscari at last, where I've longed for you to be.' He squeezed her hand. 'There, does that convince you?'

'*Ouch!*' she exclaimed, mocking him and freeing her hand from his to shake it as if he had paralysed it. 'You grip hard, Frankie!'

He recaptured her hand and raised it to his lips to kiss it.

'I asked my mother to find you many times,' he said. 'But she wouldn't do anything. She was afraid to offend my grandfather. Then last time Vittorio visited us I asked him if he would look for you while he was in London. You see, I didn't even know if you were alive, if you'd survived that awful crash.' A shudder went through him and it was Marina's turn to grip his hand tightly as she empathised with his agony of spirit. 'I used to dream about it. I still dream about it,' he said hoarsely. 'I had to find out what had happened to you. I had to know. You do understand, don't you?'

'Yes, I understand,' she replied consolingly.

'At first Vittorio refused to do as I asked. He said he would be too busy to wander about London looking for the sort of woman you are.'

'Oh?' Marina's head went up and her back stiffened. 'And just what did he mean by that? What sort of woman did he think I am?' she asked icily.

'The sort who uses her looks and her body to earn her living,' Frankie muttered. 'Sometimes he is very cynical.' He gave a short laugh. 'It was then I behaved badly, like a spoilt child. I threw a tantrum and I threatened suicide if you weren't found and brought here to see me. My mother broke down, then, and pleaded with Vittorio to do as I asked.' He laughed again. 'Oh, it was a typical Sicilian family scene—lots of shouting, lots of crying! You wouldn't have liked it at all. But Vittorio gave in, not to me, but to Mamma. He is really very fond of her and knows what a difficult time she has with Grandfather. He agreed to look for you and to give you my letter if he found you. And he went with Mamma to see Grandfather to ask permission to invite you here. Grandfather granted his permission, but I don't think he would have done if Vittorio hadn't been with Mamma.'

'I see,' murmured Marina.

His fingers brushed against her cheek caressingly.

'And now I have seen that what happened to me didn't happen to you,' he said. 'I was afraid your beautiful face might have been damaged like mine was ... and that I was to blame. Ah, *Dio mio*, Marina, will you ever forgive me for what happened that night?'

'It was an accident. It could have happened to anyone,' she said comfortingly. 'And how can I say I forgive you when I've never blamed you?'

'But if you haven't blamed me why have you never written to me?'

'I was ill for a long time and then when I got better I thought that perhaps you wouldn't want to hear from me,' she replied cautiously. It was difficult to explain without hurting his feelings too much.

'How could you think I wouldn't want to hear from you?' he growled angrily.

'You didn't write to me,' she pointed out. 'No one in your family contacted me to let me know how you were, so I just assumed that you had decided it was wiser not to have anything to do with me any more.' She paused, then asked tentatively, 'Why did you tell your uncle ... and your mother ... that you were eloping when the car crashed?'

'Because it was true.'

'I didn't know that you intended to do that. I thought you were driving me home. I didn't know you were driving to Dover with the intention of going to France until your uncle told me a few days ago. Oh, Frankie, why did you do it? Why did you go the wrong way?'

The back of the wheelchair creaked as he flung himself against it. He dropped her hand. Marina couldn't see his face properly in the dusk, but she guessed his mouth was pouting sulkily as he took exception to her remonstration.

'I wanted you,' he muttered. 'But you wouldn't take me seriously.'

'How could I? I was engaged to Steve.'

'But you didn't love him,' Frankie said shrewdly. He leaned forward again until his face was close to hers. 'You were the first woman I'd met who wasn't impressed by my wealthy connections, who seemed to like me for myself. You were the first woman who'd refused to sleep with me.'

'That was why you wanted to marry me?' she gasped.

'Partly.' His breath hissed as he drew it in. 'You were driving me crazy,' he muttered between his teeth. 'I wasn't getting anywhere with you, then suddenly at that party you loosened up a little and agreed to let me take you home. The idea of running away with you to France hit me while we were driving down the driveway from the Bentleys' house, and instead of turning right for London I turned left for Dover.'

'Your uncle says you did it to defy your grandfather because you knew he didn't approve of your friendship with me. Did you?'

'I've told you—I wanted you, that's why I did it. I was desperate. Vittorio was going to arrive at any minute and I had to do something before he arrived; before you and he met; before he. . . .' He broke off, his breath labouring harshly, and leaned forward to peer closely at her face. 'You've met him now,' he whispered viciously. 'What do you think of him? Do you find him sexy like other women do? Has *he* been able to persuade *you* to sleep with *him*? He's a master at seduction. God knows how many innocents have fallen for his satanic good looks and offhand charm.' His hand gripped hers painfully and he shook her arms. 'Has he seduced you, Marina? Has he? Has he? Answer me!'

'No, of course he hasn't!' She spoke sharply, disturbed by his display of almost hysterical jealousy. 'Now you're being silly. Signor Matissi and I were less than two hours together in London, in a restaurant most of the time, and we were only an hour and a half together today, coming here. Hardly time for us to become intimate.' Sarcasm rasped in her voice.

'Forgive me,' Francesco pleaded, his mood swinging violently from jealousy to penitence. 'Sometimes I get so frustrated because I can't behave normally any more, because I'm confined to this damned wheelchair, and so I lash out at people. Oh, Marina, I can't stand without support and I can't walk at all. I'm helpless!'

'I know how you feel,' she said comfortingly. 'I was like that too for a while, but I persevered with the exercises they gave me to do and slowly I began to walk. Don't give up, Frankie. Keep trying and one day you'll walk.'

'That's what everyone says,' he retorted bitterly, 'everyone, that is, except the American surgeon my grandfather has brought to Biscari to examine me. He says I'll only walk again if I have another operation on the lower part of my spine. There are nerves pinched there preventing me from walking.'

'So why haven't you had the operation?'

'The odds offered aren't enough,' he replied rather sulkily.

'What do you mean?'

'The surgeon can't offer a hundred per cent success. I might walk again, he says. Or I might lose what little use I have in my legs now. I've decided not to take the risk.' He paused and raising a hand pushed the hair back from her throat, his fingers lingering suggestively on her skin. 'And now that you're here,' he whispered insinuatingly, 'do you know what I want to do right now, Marina? I want to make love to you here on the loggia. I don't mean just to kiss you and touch you—I can do that.' Putting his words into action, he kissed her full on the lips and his hand swept lightly over her breast. 'You see I can do that,' he murmured. 'But I want to do more. I want to take all of you . . . damnation!'

Footsteps sounded on the steps, high spiky heels hitting the stone hard. Marina looked round, as Emilia appeared. Her back straight, her head held high, she stalked across the loggia towards the door, swung it open and entered the house. The door crashed closed behind her.

'It would seem my aunt is annoyed about something,' said Frankie with a malicious chuckle. 'I suppose Vittorio didn't come up to her expectations during their walk together. Her husband, who is about twenty years older than she is, has suddenly become impotent, so she says, and she's looking for a lover. She thinks she can revive her old affair with Vittorio.' He laughed again.

Revolted by what he was saying, Marina stood up and moved away towards the house. Immediately he followed her, the well-oiled wheels of his chair making no sound as it glided over the loggia floor, and for a moment she was reminded of a spider crawling quickly across the gossamer threads of its web towards a fly that was trapped in it. She turned quickly and found she was trapped too against the wall of the house.

'What's the matter? Why did you move away from me?' demanded Frankie. He laughed again in a sinister way. 'Never think you can get away from me. In this contraption I can move faster than you can.' He reached out, grabbed her hand and began to pull her towards him. 'You can sit on my knee, if you like,' he said. 'That way we'll be closer—much closer.'

'No! Please, Frankie, let go. I'd like to go indoors. It's growing cool out here, and I need a cardigan.'

For answer he tightened his grasp on her hand and jerked her forward. She fell across his knees, and at once his hands were on her, shifting over her breasts, fingers scrabbling at the fastenings on her blouse, pulling it undone. When the tips of his fingers touched her breast she felt another surge of revulsion. Her hands found the arms of the chair. She pushed away from him, but she couldn't stand upright because he had moved the chair again and was pressing her against the wall.

Suddenly the whole loggia was illuminated by

the beams of a car's headlights as it approached
the house. For a moment Marina saw the mask of
Francesco's face gleam bone-white, his dark eyes
glitter, then he was backing swiftly away from her.

'My grandfather,' he muttered. 'He's come to
dine with us, to meet you.'

Marina didn't stay to hear any more. Finding
herself free, she ran across the loggia, tugged open
the front door and hurried into the entrance hall.
Letting the door swing closed behind her, she
stood for a moment just inside catching her breath,
trying to calm herself.

The musical murmur of two voices talking in
Italian made her look up. Lucia and Vittorio were
coming across the hallway towards the doorway.
Marina stepped aside, realising that Lucia was on
her way to open the door to go out and greet her
father-in-law. Lucia flashed her a smile, nodded
her head and said,

'*Mi scusi, signorina.*'

Marina nodded back and turning away started
to walk rather blindly across the hallway,
determined to reach her room. She walked straight
into Vittorio, who had sidestepped to block the
way.

'What's the matter?' he asked.

'Nothing,' she retorted proudly. 'I'm going to
my room, to fetch a cardigan.'

He moved aside and she walked on, wanting to
run but forcing herself to walk as usual, easily,
gracefuly, her hips swaying, her arms swinging
casually. There was a moment of panic when she
wondered if she had chosen the wrong passage and

another when she wasn't sure which door she
should open. Was her room the second or the
third on the right? She hesitated outside the second
door. A dark shadow slid between her and the
door. Vittorio opened the door and pushed it back,
and she saw the gold-coloured carpet glowing in
lamplight, the sheen of white-painted furniture.

She gave Vittorio a quick up-from-under glance,
then stepped past him into the room. The door
closed behind her, and cautiously she looked over
her shoulder. He was standing in front of the door
and the white paint made a stark background
emphasising the darkness of his clothing, the olive
tint of his skin, the blackness of his curling hair.
Mephistopheles, the messenger from the devil. A
shudder went through her.

'I didn't ask you to come in here,' she said
coldly, tilting her chin at him. 'What do you want
now?'

His dark glance flitted over her and a faint smile
curved his lips.

'You put on a good show, Marina, and I admire
your spirit,' he said. 'But your stiff upper lip
doesn't fool me.' He stepped towards her. 'You
were in one hell of a panic when you came into the
house. Even now your face is white.' His glance
drifted down from her face to her blouse. 'What
happened out there?' he asked softly.

With one hand at her breast as she tried to
fasten buttons furtively, she turned away from him
and went over to the closet and opened it. From
a hanger on which she had draped it she took a
white shawl which her mother had crocheted for

her and with a graceful flick of her wrists and arms placed it around her shoulders.

'Why should I tell you what happened?' she retorted challengingly. She went over to the dressing table and picked up her hairbrush. Watching her reflection on the mirrors, she brushed the waves of her hair into place. They fell in gentle curves against her temples, seeming to draw attention to the clear blue-grey sheen of her eyes. 'You're only the go-between, the messenger,' she added insolently, turning to face him again. 'If you want to know what happened why don't you ask Frankie whose messenger you are?'

His mouth tightened and bone showed through the skin at his jawline.

'So if you won't tell me I'll just have to guess what happened, won't I?' he retorted. 'Since he found out he can't walk and can't pursue all his favourite activities, Frankie has been pretty hard to handle.' Heavy lids hid his eyes for a moment and the white edge of his teeth appeared as he chewed his lower lip. 'I think that perhaps I should give you some advice.'

'Oh, really?' she queried mockingly, raising her eyebrows at him and rounding her eyes. 'Frankie's relatives seem to be fond of invading the bedrooms of a house-guest to offer advice. It's not long since Aunt Emilia was here telling me what to do.'

'Emilia was here?' Vittorio looked up sharply. 'What did she say?'

'She told me what to wear and advised me how to behave in front of Grandfather Barberini. So what's your advice, Uncle Vittorio?' she challenged. 'What should I do when Frankie shows his affection for me by pawing me? Scream to you for help?' She gave him a scornful, raking glance. 'Remembering the way you behaved in a certain taxi, you're the last person I'd ask for help!'

His eyes burned like hot coals in his taut face and for a moment she had the distinct impression he would have liked to have retaliated to her taunt physically. She tensed all over, ready to do battle with him, but he turned away abruptly and strode to the door. Her shoulders sagged with relief. He was going to leave the room. She could lower her guard.

But he didn't open the door. He stood with his hand on the knob facing the door. At last he straightened his shoulders and his head went up, as if he had come to a decision. He turned to face her again. The swift storm of his anger had passed. Amusement glinted in the darkness of his eyes and a slight grin tugged at the corners of his mouth.

'We're striking sparks off each other again,' he remarked dryly, and came towards her. 'I realise I should know better than to come near you or to try and advise you, but the truth of the matter is whether you trust me or not I'm the only person around here who's in a position to help you if the situation gets beyond your control.'

'What situation?' she queried.

'The situation here ... between you and Frankie, and later, when you've met him, between you and Giovanni.'

'I can always leave, go back to London after

I've had my Mediterranean holiday,' she retorted lightly, turning away from him, back to the dressing table. Picking up her lipstick, she smoothed some on her lips, pretending his remarks hadn't disturbed her.

'But you don't have a return ticket,' Vittorio said quietly, appearing in the mirror behind her, his dark gaze intent as he watched what she was doing. He was a formidable presence in that pale silvery room—a dark angel come to warn her of dark doings? Marina resisted another shiver.

'I know I don't. But I've enough money with me to pay my return fare to England.' She put the top on the lipstick, put it down in the glass tray and turning round leaned her hips against the edge of the dresser, supporting herself with her arms, her hands resting on the top of the table. 'I'll go when I'm ready to go,' she added coolly. 'And I won't need help. I'm all grown up now, you know. I'm nearly twenty-three, and I've been handling difficult situations ever since I became a model when I was eighteen. I've been about the world, met all kinds of people, and so far I've managed to avoid getting into any sort of trouble.'

'Until you became involved with Frankie and were injured in that car crash with him,' he interrupted her softly, stepping nearer to her. 'And now you're caught in the Barberini web and you're going to find it hard to disentangle yourself.'

A chill went down her spine and her hands clenched on the edge of the dressing table. She recalled how she had compared Frankie to a spider when he had glided towards her and had

trapped her on the loggia. The next instant her lips
were curving into a smile and she was shaking her
head so that the silky blonde waves flirted about
her forehead and temples.

'What is it with you?' she asked mockingly.
'First you did your best in London to put me off
coming here, and now you're trying to frighten me
away. Why? Is it because you think I'm not good
enough for Frankie? Because I'm the sort of
woman who uses her looks and her body to earn
her living?' She saw his eyebrows come together in
a swift frown of puzzlement. 'Frankie told me, out
there on the loggia, that you refused to do as he
asked at first. You refused to look for me when
you went to London because you didn't have time
to wander about looking for "that sort of
woman".'

'I refused, yes,' he agreed. 'But I didn't tell him
why I refused. He made up the reason himself.'
His eyes were hidden briefly by their lids and his
mouth quirked wryly. 'To answer your question: I
tried to put you off coming here, and now I wish
you weren't here for purely personal reasons which
have nothing to do with the way you earn your
living.' His eyelids lifted and he looked her over
slowly, his eyes softening dangerously and sen-
suously. He took another step towards her. 'Did
you take Emilia's advice about what you should
wear?' he asked.

'Yes.' She took hold of the pleated skirt between
each finger and thumb to spread it out, then
dipped in a slight mocking curtsey. 'Do you
approve of the clothes she chose? Do you think I'm

covered up enough, Uncle Vittorio? Does this outfit make me seem decorous and submissive?'

When she straightened up from the curtsey she found she was very close to him and he was still looking at her in that frankly lustful way. She could have stepped back, out of danger, but for some reason she didn't want to. Staying where she was, she returned his gaze, looking up at him with clear shining eyes, her lips parting slightly as she found herself suddenly short of breath.

'No matter what you wear you always manage to look provocative,' he murmured, black lashes half covering his eyes as his glance went to her mouth and lingered there deliberately. His lips parted too and he licked them with the tip of his tongue as if he were either hungry or thirsty.

'Don't you mean sexy and silly?' Marina whispered. Her senses seemed to be suddenly very much alive, titillated into awareness by his nearness. But seeing him, scenting his masculinity, hearing the musical intonations of his voice, suddenly wasn't enough. She wanted to feel the pressure of his lips, the touch of his fingertips, and most of all she wanted to touch him, to caress his warm sun-beaten skin, to play with his silky black curls. Desire throbbed painfully within her, longing to be expressed.

'Sexy but not silly. Never silly,' he replied, stepping even closer so that there was no space between them at all, his chest touching the tips of her breasts, his hips thrusting against hers.

'Isn't it dangerous for you and me to be this close?' Marina whispered tauntingly. Time seemed to have stopped. Her heart thundered in her ears and her legs had begun to shake.

'Very dangerous,' he murmured, sliding his arms about her waist, and glad of his support, she lifted her ams to link her hands behind his neck. 'But who cares? I've always liked living dangerously.'

The broad, dark classically-moulded lips swooped to hers which were already open in sensual welcome. The spark he struck on touching her was bright and hot, flaring immediately into a flame of desire which was like nothing she had ever experienced before in her life. Many times she had been kissed by boy-friends when she had been younger, by Steve when she had been engaged to him, by Frankie recently on the loggia, but never until now had she wanted to kiss back, to respond wholeheartedly and to make her own passionate demands; to give of herself recklessly and never count the cost. Consumed by the flame of desire, she became the flame herself, instinctively using her lips, her hands, her whole body to express passion and to arouse it in him.

It ended suddenly. With his hands hard on her shoulders, Vittorio thrust her away from him. Breathless, his eyes smouldering still with desire, he stared at her for a moment, then his hands dropped to his sides and he stepped back. The heavy lids hid his eyes again and the wry twist appeared at the corner of his mouth.

'That was quite a performance,' he drawled. 'Now I understand why Frankie was so desperate for you to come here. Now I know why he's so keen to have you share his bed.' He turned towards the door again. 'I must go,' he muttered, 'or I'll miss the ferry back to Catania.'

'You . . . you're leaving tonight?' Still trembling from the flare-up of passion, Marina leaned against the dressing table again, holding on to it as if her very life depended on it.

'I'm leaving now,' he said from the doorway. 'I have to work tomorrow.' He slanted her a sideways glance. '*Arrivederci,* Marina. Enjoy your Mediterranean holiday—and good luck,' he said softly.

The door opened and closed. He had gone, and she was alone with his final sardonic remarks about her return of his kiss ringing in her ears, mocking her. Slowly she turned and looked at herself in the mirror. What had happened to her? Why at his touch had she thrown aside the prudence which had always protected her until now? Why had she shown him, of all people, the depths of the hungry yearning for love that lurked beneath her cool and often mocking behaviour?

Her cheeks flushed red suddenly as she stared at herself. The sight of the blush amazed her. She had never been given to blushing, so why was she blushing now? Was it because she was ashamed of having revealed herself to a man who didn't really want to have anything to do with her; who regarded her as a fortune-hunter, a woman on the make, and who now believed she kissed any man in the same way she had just kissed him? She covered her cheeks with her hands trying to cool them and stared at herself with troubled eyes. Why, oh, why had she let him break through her guard?

Someone knocked on the door and she turned almost guiltily to look at it. Quickly she looked back at her reflection. Her lips were smudged. She picked up a tissue and rubbed the smudged lipstick from them. The knock was repeated and the door eased open slowly. Picking up her lipstick, Marina looked over her shoulder. Emilia appeared in the doorway. In a short, simple black dress with her black hair coiled into a smooth chignon she was Italian elegance personified, reminding Marina somewhat of Sophia Loren.

'I've been sent to tell you that my father is here and would like you to come and be introduced to him before we have dinner,' she said coldly. 'Are you ready?'

'Not quite,' replied Marina, her nerves picking up hostile vibrations from the woman who stood staring at her critically. 'But you don't have to wait for me.'

'*Fai presto!*' snapped Emilia, making no attempt this time to be friendly or conciliatory. 'Hurry up! My father does not like to be kept waiting.'

'Well, there's always a first time for everything, isn't there?' retorted Marina cheekily. 'Even for the Giovanni Barberinis of this world. He'll just have to wait until I'm ready to come.'

Across the room she stared challengingly at Emilia. The woman glared back, then with a slight shrug of her shoulders she began to step out of the room, drawing the door closed.

'You'll find us in the entrance hall,' she said, and shut the door.

Hardly had the door clicked shut than Marina swirled away from the dressing table towards the closet. With eager hands she pulled the blue dress from its hanger. In a few seconds, adept at quick changing, she flung off the green blouse and the grey skirt and slid the blue dress over her head. Returning to the mirror, she hid the ravages done to her lips by Vittorio's, brushed her hair once more and then draping the shawl about her shoulders she left the room and walked towards the entrance hall.

As soon as she left the dimness of the passageway Frankie saw her and glided swiftly across the floor towards her. He was dressed in a silky white shirt patterned with tiny blue flowers and wore a red and white neckerchief tied in a cheeky knot inside the open collar of the shirt. His straight black hair was brushed smoothly and in the white mask of his repaired face his dark grey eyes glittered with life.

'You look beautiful,' he whispered, and taking one of her hands raised it to his lips. 'But where did you go?' he demanded autocratically in a hoarse whisper. 'Why did you run away like that?'

'I felt chilly, so I went to get my shawl,' Marina pulled the shawl about her closely. 'And to change my clothes so that I'd look my best to meet your grandfather,' she added, looking beyond him to the group of people who were sitting on the sofas and talking.

'And did Vittorio help you to change?' Frankie's voice growled maliciously, and he tugged at her hand. She looked down at him warily.

'What do you mean?' she asked.

'Emilia says she saw him leaving your room. What was he doing in there?'

'He . . . he'd come to tell me your grandfather was waiting to meet me and to say goodbye before he left to go back to Catania,' she replied as smoothly as she could.

'He didn't have to go right into your room to do that,' he said jealously.

'He was there only a minute,' she lied. 'And he's gone now, back to Catania.'

'Thank God,' said Frankie fervently. 'And by the time he comes back everything will be settled.' His hand tightened on hers. 'Come now, and meet my grandfather.'

Giovanni Barberini was a thickset man with silvery-grey hair. His square face had been tanned by a hot sun over many years so that the skin looked like creased yellowish-brown leather. Dark eyes, small and sharp, set under bristling black eyebrows stared at Marina critically, and she was reminded again of spiders. This was the big spider sitting at the centre of the web of his family business, directing everyone and making sure that none of the flies caught in the web ever escaped.

'I am pleased to meet you at last, *signorina*,' he said, rising politely to his feet when Frankie introduced her. 'I hope you will have a pleasant stay on Biscari.'

'Thank you. It was kind of Francesco and his mother to invite me,' replied Marina, and felt Frankie squeeze her hand in appreciation of what she had said.

'I would like you to meet Dr Howard Spender from New York. Dr Spender is at present a guest in my home,' Giovanni continued in his stiff way. 'This is Miss Marina Gregson, Howard.'

'How are you?' Dr Spender was a tall fair man. His hair was cut very short and close to his scalp and shaded glasses covered his eyes. His smile was bland, noncommittal. His right hand closed powerfully around hers and the fingers squeezed hard. 'And this is my daughter Bonnie, Miss Gregson. Ever since she knew you were expected she's talked of nothing else but your fame as a photographer's model.'

'Hi.' Bonnie Spender was big, blonde and bouncy and about eighteen years of age. Her blue eyes sparkled with enthusiasm and the plain white, sleeveless dress she was wearing showed off her golden-skinned muscular arms. 'This is fantastic!' she gushed as she shook Marina's hand heartily. 'Meeting you, I mean,' she went on when Marina gave her a startled glance. 'A real live cover girl. And you really look like your photographs. I'm so glad you've come here. Do you play tennis? There are some good courts here at Frankie's place, but there's no one for me to play with. . . .'

'Marina has come to play with me, not with you,' Frankie interrupted rudely and rather jealously. He pulled on Marina's hand again. 'Let's go into the dining room. *Mamma mia* says dinner is ready to serve.'

The dining room was a long room with three arched windows through which could be seen the starlit sky. The table was set with a white cloth.

Cutlery and glassware gleamed opulently in candlelight shed from two magnificent silver candelabra.

Giovanni sat at the head of the table in a high-backed chair of carved oak upholstered in red leather which was trimmed with brass studs. Marina sat on a similar chair, not so high in the back and without arms, on his left. Frankie was next to her in his wheelchair and beyond him was Bonnie. Opposite to Marina was Howard Spender. Emilia was next to him and Lucia sat at the end of the table opposite to her father.

Two young men with sleek black hair and impassive sallow faces waited on the table quietly yet efficiently. First there was a tasty *antipasto* of fresh shellfish, then a *primo piatti* of some sort of soup which Frankie told Marina was made of pasta in broth with egg yolks and grated cheese. This was followed by veal cutlets served with *fiori di zucchini*. There was wine, a sparkling light red one.

Giovanni made no effort to converse either with Marina or with Howard Spender during the meal, seeming to be more interested in eating his food slowly and with relish. Aware that Frankie was bickering noisily with Bonnie, Marina talked with Howard Spender about New York, where she had been once for a fashion show, about London where he had spent some time when he had been a medical student and then about the injuries she had sustained in the car crash and how they had been treated.

A dessert of fresh fruit, cheese and coffee had

been served when Bonnie Spender raised her voice suddenly and furiously.

'Well, I think you're chicken!' she blurted, and everyone else stopped talking to look at her. Her face was flushed pink and her eyes were glittering, it could have been with unshed tears. 'I also think you're terribly spoilt, and I'm not a bit sorry for you just because you can't walk!'

'Bonnie!' Howard Spender's voice was sharp. 'That's no way to speak to Frankie. Remember he's our host for the evening.'

'I don't care!' Bonnie cried stormily, and turned on Frankie, who was sitting braced in his chair, his seamed and patched face livid, his dark eyes blazing. 'You're a coward, Frankie, a whining, bitter coward! And I really believe you're secretly enjoying being a cripple because it gives you a feeling of power to have us all rushing to obey your silly commands. That's why you don't want another operation. You're afraid it might be successful and you'll be able to walk again and you'll lose that power and. . . .'

'Bonnie, that's enough!' Howard's voice was icy now and behind his tinted glasses his eyes were glaring at his daughter. 'Apologise to Fr nkie and to Signora Barberini now!'

'No, I won't,' said the American girl stubbornly, and jumping to her feet she left the table and rushed from the room.

Howard pushed back his chair and rose to his feet.

'Excuse me, everyone, please,' he said, tossing down his table napkin. 'Signore, Signorina,

Frankie—all of you, I apologise on Bonnie's behalf. I really don't know what came over her, I. . . .'

'Go after her.' The gruff order came from Giovanni. 'Tell her she has only put into words what some of us have been thinking for a while but have hesitated to say to Francesco.'

At this point Frankie exploded into speech, into quick vicious Italian, and Lucia raised her voice too. Emilia joined in and the three voices jangled together while Howard Spender left the room in search of his outspoken daughter. Marina raised her coffee cup to her lips and sipped, trying to behave as if all hell hadn't been let loose around her.

'Stia quierto!' Giovanni's voice cracked like a whip, causing Marina to jump in her seat. Quickly she set down her cup in its saucer. Frankie, Lucia and Emilia all became silent together, all of them glancing rather fearfully, she thought, at the broad-shouldered, grey-haired man at the head of the table. His leathery face impassive, he let his bright dark eyes flicker over them. Then very quietly he began to issue instructions in Italian.

Wiping her mouth on her napkin, her plump sallow face suddenly drawn, Lucia rose to her feet and leaving the end of the table walked round behind Frankie's chair and began to pull it out from the table.

'Excuse me, Marina,' Frankie whispered hoarsely. 'My grandfather says he wishes to speak to you alone. I will see you later.'

Lucia pushed the wheelchair across the room

and out into the entrance hall. Standing at her place, Emilia hesitated, giving Marina a suspicious glance before she said something in Italian to Giovanni. By way of answer he waved his hand dismissingly and, after giving Marina another sharp, almost vindictive look, Emilia turned away with a shrug of her shoulders and walked out of the room. One of the young waiters appeared, to pour more coffee, then disappeared. Giovanni produced a long Havana cigar.

'It will not offend you if I smoke, *signorina*?' he asked.

'What would you do if I said yes, it would?' replied Marina determined to show him that he did not frighten her. His thin lips twitched into a faint smile.

'I would not smoke, of course,' he said. 'Like Howard's young daughter, you are not afraid to say what you think. So tell me, will it offend you if I light this cigar? Smoking one of them a day in the evening is the only vice, perhaps I should say the only extravagance, I allow myself now that I am an old man.'

'No, it won't offend me,' she said quickly, thinking how clever he was, flattering her a little by deferring to her wishes, softening her attitude by his reference to his age and his one pleasure.

When the cigar was lit and going to his satisfaction he leaned back in his chair and studied her with slitted dark eyes.

'You are a very pretty woman, *signorina*,' he said at last. 'And having now met you I can understand why my grandson is attracted to you. I was listening to what you were telling Dr Spender about your recovery from the injuries you sustained.' He paused, frowning a little, then added rather sadly, 'I wish my grandson had the same determination to walk again as you had.'

'Frankie was much more seriously hurt than I was,' Marina explained. 'And I can understand and sympathise with his refusal to have another operation. He must be tired of being mauled about. Also, he told me, there is a chance that it might not be successful and that he might . . . well, he might be worse off, not better.'

'It would be successful,' stated Giovanni forcefully. 'Spender is the best surgeon money can buy. At the price he asks he would not dare to fail. If he did fail in this case he knows that he would suffer in his profession.' The square leathery face was grim. 'I would see to it that he did,' he added in soft silky tones, and Marina felt the hairs on her neck prickle. 'But his daughter is right. Francesco is a coward and spoilt into the bargain.' Giovanni's lips twisted disgustedly. 'He is encouraged in his weakness by his mother. It is her fault he seems spoilt and seems to be content to remain crippled. Since he has been hurt she has pampered every whim of his.' Giovanni tapped the lit end of his cigar slowly and watched the thick ring of grey ash fall from it into a cut glass ash tray. Then lifting his eyes he looked directly at Marina, his eyes sharp and penetrating.

'Did you know that Francesco has threatened twice to end his life?' he queried softly.

'You mean he's tried to commit suicide?' gasped

Marina. 'Oh, how awful! He must have felt really depressed about his condition,' she whispered.

'Maybe,' the old man murmured with a touch of dryness. 'The last time he only desisted when he had extracted a promise from his mother that she would try and find you and bring you out here.' He tapped more ash from his cigar into the ashtray. 'Miss Gregson, before we go any further I would like you to know I care very much for Francesco. He is my heir and I would like him to be healthy again, as much in mind as in body. The injuries he has sustained have damaged his mind also, and only when he can walk again will he be free from the bitterness and frustration which are influencing him now. He must be persuaded somehow to have that operation. I had hoped that Howard would have been able to persuade him— that is why I invited Howard and his daughter to stay for a while on Biscari—but so far Francesco has resisted. Now you are here and I am hoping you'll use your influence over him to get him to agree to travel to Switzerland to the clinic where Howard is one of the consultant surgeons and to have the operation performed there.'

'I'll do my best, in the two weeks I'll be staying here,' said Marina, 'but don't count too much on my being able to influence him one way or the other.'

'Two weeks?' Giovanni glanced at her sharply. 'Why only two weeks?'

'I couldn't possibly impose upon Signora Barberini's hospitality longer than that,' she explained. 'Besides, I'll have to go back to

England to look for a job. I've been out of work since the accident and. . . .'

'I told Lucia to invite you to stay here for as long as it takes you to persuade Frankie to agree to have that operation,' he interrupted her rudely. 'Didn't she make that clear to you?'

'No . . . although Frankie did say I could stay as long as I like, but. . . .'

'You do not need a job in England when you can stay here for as long as you like,' he interrupted her again. 'Your job is here, to be with Francesco. You promised to marry him before that accident. You were eloping together.'

'I did not promise to marry him and I didn't know he was eloping with me,' protested Marina vehemently. 'Oh, how many times do I have to say it? Frankie asked me to marry him, but I thought he was joking and I didn't say I would marry him. I didn't agree to elope with him either.'

'That isn't the way he tells the story,' Giovanni said at his driest. 'And he still wants to marry you. He will probably propose to you in the next few days.'

'Oh, dear!' sighed Marina ruefully.

'And in view of his condition you'll find it difficult to refuse him, won't you?' suggested Giovanni smoothly, and she looked up to find him watching her with his small dark eyes. 'You'll hesitate to turn down his proposal in case he threatens to do away with himself again, won't you?'

'Yes, I suppose I will,' she muttered. 'I wouldn't

want him to think that I was refusing because . . . well, because he's crippled.'

'Of course you wouldn't. So may I suggest what you might say to him?' asked Giovanni, and she nodded. 'I suggest,' he continued, 'that you say you'll only agree to marry him if he agrees to go to Switzerland to have the operation first.'

Her eyes wide, Marina stared at him in silence. The beady eyes stared back at her.

'But supposing Frankie agrees to have the operation,' she said at last, 'and it's successful. What then? Will I have to marry him?'

'I have always believed in crossing a bridge only when I come to it, *signorina*,' he replied coolly. 'Through you it is possible for us to rescue Francesco from his crippled condition. He must be persuaded somehow to agree to have that operation, and I think that can be done by you refusing to marry him unless he has it.' He leaned towards her. 'I can assure you that if you go along with this suggestion of mine and he does agree to have the operation my daughter-in-law and I will always be grateful to you, whatever the outcome. Will you try to do what I ask, to help Francesco?'

She was trapped. If she refused to do what he suggested she would always feel guilty for not having tried to help Frankie. And yet to agree was to entangle herself further in the Barberini web, and she might end up marrying a man she didn't love.

'You did say you'd do your best to help,' Giovanni prompted softly. 'And I don't believe you're the sort of person who goes back on her word. Again I ask you. Will you try to do what I ask, to help Francesco?'

Marina thought of Frankie as he had been when she had first met him, lively, and boyish. Then she thought of him as he was now, bitter and frustrated.

'I'll try,' she said simply.

CHAPTER FOUR

WARM spring sunshine slanted over the feathery tops of the row of tall cypresses which edged a courtyard at the back of the Barberini villa. In elegantly carved plant vases, carved from pale gold stone, the flowers of creeping geraniums glowed pink and red and their velvety green leaves trailed on slender stems almost to the ground. Birds of all sorts and sizes swooped down to the courtyard to visit the bird table in one corner.

It was almost eleven o'clock in the morning, and as usual at that time Marina and Frankie were drinking coffee which had been brought to them by a small maidservant. Frankie was, as always, seated in his wheelchair and Marina was sitting on one of the wooden seats which had been inserted into the stone wall that edged the courtyard. The evening before they had both been guests with Lucia at a dinner given by Giovanni, and now Frankie seemed determined to discuss the other people who had been at the dinner.

'I was surprised Aunt Emilia was there, though,' he said. 'I'd have thought she would have stayed longer in Catania.'

'Oh, has she been staying there?' Marina asked indifferently. It was her sixth day on the island and she had to admit that so far she had enjoyed every moment of her holiday. Lucia had treated her with kindness and civility, the servants in the villa had been friendly and pleasant, Bonnie Spender had turned out to be a cheerful and lively companion both on the tennis courts and on the donkey rides they had taken together; and Frankie had been on his best behaviour, never once attempting to make love to her again and never once suggesting marriage or any other liaison, so that she had begun to think that Giovanni and Victor had both been wrong in assuming that Frankie still wanted to marry her.

'Didn't you know?' Frankie said now. 'She left Biscari last Saturday as soon as she realised Vittorio wouldn't be coming back here for a while.' He laughed rather maliciously. 'And she came face to face with Gina Cortesi, so she retreated in haste and came back to Biscari yesterday.'

Marina said nothing. She had learned during the past week that Frankie liked nothing better than to gossip about his family. He liked particularly to make disparaging remarks about Vittorio, giving her the impression that his uncle was immoral in his dealings with women; a rake who caused his mother and his sisters a great deal of worry because he showed no signs of getting married and settling down to raise a family.

'You're supposed to ask who Gina Cortesi is,' Frankie prompted her rather sulkily.

'Why?' she asked, raising her eyebrows at him.

'So that I can tell you about her, of course,' he said, his lips twitching into a reluctant grin. 'Oh, you're no fun to gossip with, Marina,' he complained.

'That's because I don't like gossip,' she replied serenely. 'I like to form my own opinion about the people I meet and not to listen to gossip about them.'

'So what is your opinion of Uncle Vittorio?' he demanded, turning to gaze at her with sharp penetrating eyes.

'I've told you, I wasn't with him long enough to get to know him very well,' she retorted warily.

'And Aunt Emilia? What do you think of her?'

'She . . . well, she seems to be unhappy. I think that perhaps she's had many disappointments in her life.'

'You're right there,' said Frankie. 'She has. And the biggest one was her not being able to marry Vittorio.' He gave her another sly glance. 'Since you're not going to ask me who Gina Cortesi is I'm going to tell you. She's Vittorio's secretary, but we all know she is much more than a secretary to him. You know what I mean?' he added slyly.

'I suppose you're trying to tell me that Gina Cortesi is your uncle's mistress as well as his secretary,' she said coolly.

'Right first time,' he said with a chuckle. 'Of course none of us knows for sure that she is, but it seems that way. I mean, she doesn't live in his house with him. I suppose he could hardly have her there to live with him seeing that his mother and his youngest sister still live there. . . . Where are you going?'

Marina had risen to her feet, not wanting to hear any more of his gossip. Immediately he moved in his chair, preventing her from leaving him.

'I'm going to change into my tennis clothes,' she replied smoothly. 'Bonnie will be here soon to play.'

'Not yet. She won't be here yet,' he said. He reached out and took one of her hands, his manner changing swiftly. 'Please sit down, Marina,' he said coaxingly. 'There's something I want to ask you.'

'You promise not to gossip any more about your uncle or your aunt?' she said, frowning down at him severely. 'I really find them rather boring, and I'm not at all interested in their private lives.'

'All right, I promise.' His dark glittering glance swept over her possessively. 'As always you're looking very lovely. The sunshine of the last few days has given colour to your face. Are you enjoying being here on Biscari?'

'Yes, I am.' She sat down again. He continued to hold her hand. 'Your mother has been very kind.'

'And so have I?' he asked eagerly, leaning towards her. 'Please say I have, Marina. I've tried very hard to behave myself and not to offend you because I wanted you to stay with me.'

'And so have you,' she replied accommodatingly.

'Everyone has been so nice to me that it's going to be hard for me to leave.'

'Leave?' he exclaimed, frowning. 'Why are you talking of leaving? I told you in my letter to you that if you came you could stay as long as you like.'

'I know you did. Your invitation was very generous, but I can't stay here longer than two weeks. I'll have to leave at the end of next week to go back to England to look for a job.'

He stared at her, puzzlement flickering in his eyes.

'But Grandfather said last night that you. . . .' he broke off to scowl at her warily and to chew at his lower lip. Then his scowl faded and he smiled at her. 'Grandfather likes you. He likes you very much.'

'How do you know he does?'

'I know because last night when I told him I want to marry you he gave me permission to propose to you.' He leaned towards her again eagerly. 'I wanted to marry you before the accident, only you wouldn't take me seriously. I still want to marry you. That's why I invited you to come and stay here, to meet my family, to see where I live. I knew that once they had met you Grandfather and Mamma would like you and find you acceptable, and now I hope you will take me seriously. Marina, please will you marry me?'

She sat in stunned silence feeling the soft warm air fan her face, smelling the delicate scent of jasmine whose tiny yellow flowers starred the low wall, hearing the birds chirping among the trees.

From the house came the sound of a tenor voice raised in song; one of the manservants singing a Neapolitan love-song.

'I don't know what to say,' she muttered, looking down at Frankie's slender long fingers grasping her hand.

'Say yes, you'll marry me,' he urged her, with a laugh. 'Please say yes, and we'll be married here in Biscari soon.'

There had been times during the past week when Marina had thought she might accept his proposal ... if he ever proposed, arguing that marriage to the heir to the Barberini fortune would solve her immediate problem of not having a job. Marriage to Frankie would provide her with all the security she could ever need. As long as she stayed with him, behaved as a good wife should, she would be able to live in luxury for the rest of her life, like Emilia Rossi had lived with her husband, and maybe by the time she was Emilia's age she would look like her, elegantly dressed, sophisticated, but with a sour twist to her mouth, her eyes dark and hollow with discontent because after all she hadn't married for love.

'I can't,' she whispered, still looking down. 'I can't say yes, I'll marry you.'

'Why? Why can't you? What is stopping you?' Frankie's voice rose excitedly, reminding her she was treading on treacherous ground. 'It's because I can't walk? Because I ... I ... look ugly?' he whispered.

'No, oh, no,' she said quicky, looking up and remembered what Giovanni had suggested she should say. If she didn't want to hurt Frankie's feelings too much she should say she would only agree to marry him if he would agree to have another operation so he could walk again. 'I . . . I can only promise to marry you if you'll promise to do something for me first,' she said steadily.

'What do you want me to do?' he demanded.

'I . . . I'd like you to agree to let Dr Spender operate.'

'So I was right,' he grated through set teeth and from under sullen brows his eyes glittered at her angrily. Letting go of her hand, he flung himself back in his chair. 'You don't want to marry me because I'm crippled!'

'I didn't say that,' she retorted, realising that she was handling the whole business very badly. 'I . . . I . . . said I'll promise to marry you as soon as you promise to have another operation. Oh, Frankie, don't you want to walk again? Do you want to spend the rest of your life in a wheelchair?'

He stared at her for a moment, then covered his face with both hands.

'Ah, *Dio´ mio*, how could you do this to me? How could you be so cruel?' he muttered brokenly. Lifting his face, he glared at her again. 'And I believed you liked me. I believed you came here because you like me and want to be with me.'

'I do like you. I've always liked you, but I don't like what you're becoming,' she murmured. 'Please, for your own sake agree to have that operation and I . . . I promise I'll marry you when it's over and you're walking again.'

Narrow and sharp, like Giovanni's, his eyes studied her face.

'But supposing the operation is a failure and I'm not able to walk again, what then?' he challenged her. 'Will you stand by your promise and marry me?'

'Yes,' she whispered, but was unable to look him in the eyes.

'Blackmailer!' He spat out the word viciously and she looked up quickly and defensively. 'My God,' he went on, 'to think that you whom I've loved and worshipped ever since I set eyes on you could stoop to blackmail!'

'I'm not blackmailing you. I . . . I'm trying to help you, give you a good reason for wanting to have the operation and to walk again,' she argued quietly.

'I see. If I'm a good boy and do what you ask and have the operation, I'll get you as a reward,' Frankie said nastily. 'I wish I knew who had put you up to this,' he added shrewdly, and Marina had difficulty in controlling her start of surprise at his astuteness.

'Hi, you two!' Bonnie's voice called to them across the courtyard. Dressed in tennis whites, her sun-tanned skin gleaming like oiled silk, she seemed to bounce across the yard towards them, her hair shining glossily, her blue eyes dancing with the pure joy of being alive. 'My, you do look serious!' she chaffed them. 'Time for tennis, Marina.'

'Go away!' Frankie shouted at her. He hadn't forgiven her for her outspokenness at dinner the first evening Marina had been on the island and usually avoided meeting her when she came to the villa, making no effort to hide his resentment of her friendliness with Marina. 'Go away and play tennis by yourself.'

'But Marina promised yesterday she would play with me again today,' Bonnie began, when Frankie swung his chair round and advanced on her, propelling the chair as fast as he could as if he intended to run her down, and she had to jump to one side to avoid him.

'I've asked Marina to marry me,' he said defiantly, bringing his chair to a stop and turning to face the bewildered American girl.

'Oh.' Some of the joy seemed to go out of Bonnie. She looked strangely deflated, seemed to grow smaller. 'Really?' she queried, looking at Marina.

'Really,' Frankie snapped, not giving Marina a chance to answer.

'When is the wedding to be?' Bonnie asked.

'It would be next week if I could have my own way,' Frankie growled sulkily. 'But she says she won't agree to marry me until I've agreed to have that other operation. She's blackmailing me. What do you think of that?'

'I think it's great,' said Bonnie, brightening visibly and smiling encouragingly at Marina. 'Good for you, Marina. Are you going to do it, Frankie? Are you going to have the operation? Oh, I do hope you are!'

'So that your father will be paid the big fat fee my grandfather has offered him, I suppose,'

Frankie said sneeringly, and Bonnie's face went white. She looked as if she would burst into tears.

'Oh, you're vile, absolutely vile, do you know that?' she blurted childishly. 'And I hate you. I'm sure Marina is welcome to have you as a husband. I wouldn't marry you even if you were the fastest thing on two legs! You're mean and spiteful and . . . Oh!' She turned and ran from the courtyard along the path to the tennis court, her bare legs flashing under her short white tennis skirt.

'That wasn't a very nice thing to say to her,' Marina rebuked Frankie sharply.

'But it was true. Spender is interested in the fee Grandfather has offered him.'

'Maybe he is, but I'm sure that hasn't occurred to Bonnie. She cares for you very much and wants you to walk again as much as I do.'

'She has a damned funny way of showing she cares,' he muttered. 'She's always picking on me, nagging at me.' He slanted a narrow suspicious glance at her. 'And her father *is* being blackmaled into performing another operation on me, as much as you're blackmailing me now to have him perform it.'

Marina stared at him, her heart twisting with pity for him as she saw suddenly how frightened he was; so frightened that he had become suspicious of anyone who wouldn't let him have his own way.

'Frankie, please, you mustn't think like that about any of us,' she said in a low voice. 'All of us, your grandfather, Dr Spender, Bonnie, me . . . we're all trying to do our best to help you, but you're not being very co-operative.'

'If you want to help me you'll marry me, Marina,' he whispered. 'Marry me and I swear to you that I'll try hard to learn to walk again. Once I know you're mine I'll feel different, I know I will. I want you, Marina. I ache for you. Please say you'll marry me!'

His possessive attitude alarmed her, roused her freedom-loving spirit. She guessed he didn't love her for herself but only for what she appeared to be ... a cover girl, 'sexy but silly'—Vittorio Matissi's sardonic comment echoed through her mind. Frankie wanted her—or rather coveted her, as he might covet a beautiful painting or ornament belonging to someone else. He wanted her because so far he hadn't been able to have her, because she had refused to take him seriously and wouldn't let him make love to her. At heart he was a pirate like his Saracen ancestors, like his grandfather Giovanni, and when he saw something he wanted he would do everything he could to get it so that he could show it off to the rest of the world. He wanted her for the same reason, so he could show her off and say, *Look at the beautiful wife I managed to get even though I'm crippled and my face has been damaged. Aren't you jealous? Don't you wish you were me?*

'Marina, what is it? Why are you looking at me like that?' His voice, hoarse and a little desperate, broke into her horrified thoughts, scattering them. Marina shook her head and laughed a little.

'I'm sorry,' she replied. 'I was just thinking ahead,' she added quickly, suddenly seeing a way to answer his proposal negatively without hurting him too much. 'I was thinking,' she whispered, not looking at him, 'how awful it would be if . . . if I married you now and then one day in the future when you're fully recovered and can walk again you'll wish you hadn't married me.'

'Marina, you're not making sense,' he argued.

'Well, it's hard to put into words . . . but I think you're only asking me to marry you now because you think I'll do it because I'm sorry for you.'

'And aren't you sorry for me?' he challenged her.

'Yes, I am, but . . . but that isn't a good enough reason for me to give in to you and say I'll marry you now. It would be much better if you could wait and propose to me again after you've had that operation and can walk again.'

'But don't you understand, I don't think I can wait any longer,' he groaned. 'Oh, you don't know what it's like wanting to make love to you and not being able to because you won't . . . you won't. . . .' he broke off to swing his chair away from her. After a while he said in a choked voice, 'All right. I agree. I'll see Dr Spender this afternoon and ask him how soon the operation can be done.' The chair swung round again so that he faced her again. 'But you've got to promise to stay with me until I have it. You're to travel with me to Switzerland, be there with me when I go under the anaesthetic, be there when I come out of it,' he said arrogantly. 'I'm going to make sure of that.'

'How can you?' she retorted, her rebellious spirit rising again. 'How can you stop me from leaving if I want to leave?'

'You'll see,' he replied tautly, his eyes glittering

with malice. 'Now where are you going?' She
stood up.

'To play tennis with Bonnie, of course. She must
be getting tired of waiting for me,' she said
serenely. She let her hand rest lightly on his
shoulder. 'I'm so glad you've decided to reconsider
having the operation, and I promise I'll stay with
you until you have it.'

Frankie seized hold of her hand and pressed hot
lips against it, then together they moved towards
the house.

'Don't say anything to Bonnie yet,' he ordered.
'I want to make sure of the date the operation can
be done and of all the necessary arrangements
before making an announcement.'

'I won't say anything to anyone,' she agreed.

The argument with Frankie had made great
demands on her resources, she found, and she
played a rather lifeless game of tennis, losing as
always to the athletic bouncing Bonnie, who
seemed to have remained amazingly unaffected by
her violent disagreement with Frankie.

'Did you really mean it when you said you'd
only agree to marry Frankie if he goes through
with the operation?' Bonnie asked Marina as they
walked away from the court when the game was
over.

'Yes, I really meant it.'

'I think you're awfully strong . . . I don't mean
physically but spiritually. I mean, you have the
strength not to give in to him. If . . . if he'd asked
me to marry him I'd have said yes straight away.'

'You would?' Marina stopped in her tracks and

turned to stare in amazement. 'Why?'

'Oh, 'cos I'm crazy about him, I suppose,' muttered Bonnie, her face going pink, her eyelashes fluttering down shyly over her eyes.

'But you're always fighting with him,' gasped Marina. 'You're always so rude to him, and he's most unpleasant to you.'

'I know,' Bonnie sighed. 'I guess I'm rude to him because if I weren't I . . . well, I'd show my real feelings for him, and what would be the use of that? He's in love with you and doesn't care that much for me.' She snapped her fingers. 'Do you think he'll have the operation?' she asked next, giving Marina a curious glance.

'I don't know. He wouldn't commit himself,' replied Marina cautiously.

'And now I'm in a worse mix-up than ever,' muttered Bonnie. 'You see, I do want him to have that operation because I know it will be successful and he'll walk again. But if he has it now, he and you will get married, and then. . . .' Bonnie broke off to sniff, her eyes sparkling with tears. 'Oh, Marina, I wish you weren't quite so lovely and generous. I wish I could dislike you, but I can't. Oh, why did you have to come here? If you hadn't come there might have been a chance for me with Frankie. If you'd refused his invitation he might have turned to me for friendship instead. I wish you hadn't come!'

Turning, Bonnie rushed away round the side of the house, and after a moment Marina went indoors to her room to change out of the white skirt and T-shirt she had worn to play tennis. She put on pale pink jeans belted at the waist and a darker pink cotton shirt, then went through to the dining room where she ate lunch with Lucia, Frankie having chosen to eat in his private sitting room. After lunch, feeling a need for exercise, she decided to go for a walk by herself. When she stepped from the house into the courtyard she came face to face with a young man, not too tall but powerfully built, who was wearing a plain white short-sleeved shirt, open at the neck, and dark pants. Black-haired, swarthy-skinned and black-eyed, he was a typical islander.

'*Buon giorno, signorina,*' he said. 'I am Giulio. Signor Francesco has appointed me to be your bodyguard. I must go with you everywhere,' he explained in careful heavily-accented English.

'Why?' Marina's eyes opened wide.

'He is afraid someone might try to kidnap you, *signorina.*'

'Really?' She couldn't help laughing. 'Whoever would want to kidnap me?'

'I do not know,' he replied without a glimmer of a smile. 'But sometimes it happens. Where do you go now?'

'I'm going for a walk. As far as the temple of Apollo, on the hill, up there.' She gestured towards the trees at the back of the house. 'I'm only going to look at the view. I'm afraid you're going to be very bored.'

'It does not matter. I do my job,' Giulio said seriously, shrugging his shoulders, and when she set off towards the pathway that led through the trees he moved behind her at a discreet distance.

So this was Frankie's way of making sure she wouldn't leave Biscari, thought Marina. Giulio wasn't just a bodyguard to protect her from being kidnapped. He was also there to prevent her from leaving the island without Frankie knowing.

The narrow stony path twisted up the hillside under the shade of olive trees. After a while the olive trees gave way to pine trees as the terrain became more rocky and above her, slanting upwards, glowing gold against the brilliant blue sky, she could see three marble columns supporting the broken remains of the architrave, frieze and cornice, all that was left standing of a temple which had been built long ago by the first Greek inhabitants of the island.

From the shade of the pines she emerged into the heat of the midday sun that blazed down in the jumble of marble blocks which had once formed the rest of the temple. Picking her way through the rubble of stones, she mounted the three broken steps on which the columns stood and which had once led into the interior of the temple.

Against the fluted shaft of the middle column she leaned, feeling the sun-warmed stone striking through the thinness of her blouse. On either side of the hill the land fell away, patterned by the dark green of pines and the shimmering silvery green of olive trees. Far below the sea was a deep blue, flecked with scales of silver, and in the distance the island of Sicily loomed, purple blue, the volcano Etna a brooding presence, its concave summit wreathed in a cloud of steam.

Marina frowned uneasily as she looked across

the strait of water that separated Biscari from
Sicily. Thirty miles betwen her and freedom.
Thirty miles to Catania, the airport and a plane to
London. Thirty miles she couldn't cross because
every move she made was being watched by the
young man Giulio who was somewhere behind
her, lounging in the shade cast by one of the fallen
Doric columns.

She was caught, trapped in the Barberini web as
Vittorio Matissi had predicted she would be, and all
because she had told Frankie she would agree to
marry him if he would agree to have another
operation. She shifted restlessly, frowning uneasily
again as she realised how easily she had been
manipulated not only by Giovanni Barberini but
also by Vittorio. If he hadn't appeared to be so
much against her coming to Biscari, she might not
have accepted Frankie's invitation. She had
accepted it to defy him and now she was trapped
because she had tightened the strands of the web
about herself, that morning. Why? Why hadn't she
refused to marry Frankie outright? Because she
was sorry for him and wanted to help him, that
was why.

But she didn't want to marry him. Oh, no, she
couldn't marry him, so how was she going to get
out of her promise to him if he went ahead and
had the operation and learned to walk again? How
could she refuse to marry him then and be easy in
her conscience?

She turned and looked down into the horseshoe-
shaped bay, her attention caught by a movement
down there, a flash of white. Between the two

headlands a yacht was motoring into the bay, its sunlit sails shaking and shimmering. Leaving the column against which she had been leaning, Marina went down the steps and walked round to the other side of the ruins so that she had a better view of the bay.

The yacht had a dark hull and two masts, the taller one being just forward of the centre of the boat, the shorter one nearer to the stern. As she stared a dark figure left the cockpit of the boat and went up on deck to the mainmast, released a halliard, and the foresail billowed down on to the foredeck. Then another halliard was released and the mainsail crumpled, sliding down the mast to lie in folds on the cabin roof.

The yacht was a ketch, she had no doubts about that, and Vittorio Matissi owned a ketch. Was it his yacht? Had he come back to Biscari? Her heart leapt and began to beat fast. Her pulses raced and the scene before her blurred. She saw instead a dark lean face. Brown eyes slanted a downward sidelong glance at her from under black lashes. Broad firmly moulded lips parted in a slight provocative smile.

Impatiently she shook her head to shake away the image and the bay and the headlands came into sharp focus again. But the yacht had gone, and for a moment she wondered whether it, like Vittorio Matissi's face, had been a figment of her imagination, a product perhaps of wishful thinking, because subconsciously she had been hoping and wishing that Vittorio Matissi would return to the island. Then she noticed the darker ripple on the blue water of the bay, the wake left by the passing of a boat, and realised the yacht had been hidden from her view by the green curve of the land.

She had thought about Vittorio a lot since she had left the island the previous Friday. She had thought about him far too much. She had even found herself reliving the moments she had spent with him, going over their arguments, indulging in romantic fantasies about him, only to berate herself later for foolishness, telling herself that he had probably forgotten all about her.

Oh, why waste time thinking about a man she had disliked as soon as she had met him and who had shown he had no respect for her and who, she knew now from the various remarks Frankie had made about his uncle, had a reputation for amusing himself amorously with women, who had a mistress in Catania and probably in other cities in Europe too, if the truth were known. It was easy enough to understand why she disliked him. He had done everything he could to alienate her.

They struck sparks off each other, so it was dangerous for them to be too close to each other, he had said. Why? What was there between them? Was it just physical attraction and nothing more? Marina felt the nerves at the pit of her stomach tighten at the thought of meeting him again, of being close to him, of being able to touch him. God, what was the matter with her? She had never felt like this about a man in her life, not even about Steve, her childhood sweetheart to whom she had been engaged for a short time, and she had certainly never felt like this about Frankie.

It was as if she were possessed by an evil spirit, by a daemon lover who even when he was absent could rouse her to passion and who even now seemed to be calling her to him.

Turning suddenly, she began to walk quickly through the broken marble columns and blocks. Giulio emerged from behind his shelter.

'I'm going down to the bay,' she said to him. 'I have to go to meet someone.'

'Si, signorina.'

She was halfway down the flight of wide stone steps that led from the front of the villa down the cliffside to the sandy beach of the bay when a figure appeared at the bottom of the steps, intending to climb up them. Seeing her, he stepped back on to the sand and waited for her to approach him. On the bottom step she paused, and although her heart was singing with a strange new joy on seeing him she protected herself as usual with a pretence of indifference. Thrusting her hands into the front pockets of her pink jeans, she shook back the loose waves of her hair from her face and looked straight at him, her grey eyes clear and shining, her lips that matched exactly the dark pink shade of her blouse curving in a slight smile.

'You're the last person I expected to see here,' she lied casually.

He was standing sideways to her and he slanted a glance at her over the turned-up collar of his yellow inflatable sailing jacket. His lips quirked into a sardonic smile.

'So why did you come to meet me?' he queried softly, and Marina felt a strange thrill tingle along her nerves as she remembered how when she had been on the hill by the temple she had felt he had been calling to her. She looked past him at the dark rubber dinghy pulled up on the beach and beyond it across the glinting blue water to the graceful yacht, its yellow masts, varnished cabin roof and dark blue hull were reflected almost perfectly in the calm water.

She looked back at Vittorio. He was still looking at her, his dark eyes slanting a wary glance down at her face from beneath black lashes, his lips still parted in a slight smile; looking at her as if he knew something about her that she didn't know about herself. And suddenly the feeling that she had met him like this once before, in another life, long ago, swept over her. Thousands of years ago she had stood on a rim of pale sand and had welcomed a man who had come from the sea and had seduced him into staying with her for many years.

'Did you have a good voyage?' she asked, and immediately wondered why she had used the word voyage. He had come only thirty miles, after all.

'It was good,' he replied, not seeming in the least surprised by the word. 'I left Catania at six this morning, but I had no intention of coming here.'

'Then why did you come?'

'The wind was fair for Biscari and it just blew me this way,' he replied easily. 'Would you like to come sailing with me?'

'Now?' she exclaimed.

'*Si*. Now. It is now or never. I shall not be sailing this way again while you are here.'

'I'd love to come sailing with you,' she replied impulsively, then remembered Giulio. She glanced over her shoulder. He was halfway up the steps leaning against the handrail in the shade of the overhanging branches of a pine tree.

'Who is your friend?' Vittorio asked quietly, and she looked back at him. He was facing her now and was looking up at Giulio, and he was frowning.

'He isn't a friend. He's Giulio and he's been appointed by Frankie to keep a watch over me. He goes everywhere I go to make sure no one kidnaps me,' she replied. 'And also, I think, to make sure I don't leave the island.'

His glance swerved back to her face and he nodded. He didn't seem to be at all surprised.

'Mafia tactics?' he suggested mockingly. 'How long has this been going on?'

'Since this morning.'

He looked up again at the lounging Giulio, then said quietly, his lips hardly moving,

'Go to the dinghy. I'll be with you in a few minutes.'

'Oh, but. . . .' she began to argue.

'If you really want to go sailing with me you'll do as I say,' he said sharply, his glance swerving away from Giulio and back to her face. 'And you do want to go with me, don't you, Marina?' he added softly, his eyes appraising her in that sensual, almost lustful way that made a strange fearful excitement go tripping along her nerves.

'Yes, I do. But what about Giulio?'

'Go to the dinghy and wait for me. I'll deal with him,' he murmured.

Still she hesitated, longing to obey the impulse that urged her to go sailing with him, to run to the dinghy, yet held back by a certain innate caution which warned her that to go with him would be dangerous for her. She might get hurt beyond bearing and would never be the same again.

'You won't hurt him?' she whispered, transferring her anxiety for herself to the young man who stood waiting and watching on the steps, and she glanced up at Vittorio's dark impassive face. His lips curved back over his teeth in a grin of pure amusement.

'What do you think I am? A bully who has to use strong-arm methods all the time to get his own way?' he retorted mockingly. 'No, I won't hurt him, I promise.' He raised a hand to touch her cheek gently, his forefinger stroking the smooth sunwarmed skin caressingly as he looked down at her, a warm expression softening his eyes. 'I'll try not to hurt you too,' he murmured obscurely. 'Now go to the dinghy, Marina.'

Her will was no longer under her control. Like someone who had been hypnotised she turned and walked across the soft sand to the dinghy and waited, looking out to sea, her mind empty of all thought as she made the most of the sensory pleasures offered by the afternoon; the dazzle of sunbeams on blue water, the sigh of little waves sucking at the sand, the scents of pines, olives and many flowers mingling together.

Vittorio came silently to the dinghy and without a word pushed it down the slope of the shore to the water, bow first. He stepped into it and when he was settled on the centre thwart she followed him, her pants pulled up well above her ankles, her shoes in one hand, and took her seat on the small wooden wedge that formed the stern thwart.

It was good to be on the water again, to feel the problems associated with being on land easing away from her. The sea breeze lifted her hair and cooled her skin. Vittorio rowed with short swift strokes and the air-filled dinghy bobbed lightly over the ruffled water. They didn't speak nor did they look at each other. It was as if neither of them wished to break the spell of mesmeric silence; as if each of them feared to see what was expressed in the other's eyes.

The dinghy angled in to the hull of the yacht, nudging against it like a small animal nudges its snout against its mother. Knowing what was expected of her, Marina stood up and heaved herself on to the deck of the yacht. She stepped down into the cockpit, looking around her with interest at the varnished wooden coamings, the dark blue vinyl-covered seat cushions, the carved wooden steering wheel on its pedestal.

Vittorio tied the dinghy's painter to a cleat on the afterdeck and the little boat floated backwards behind the stern of the yacht. He stepped down into the cockpit, reached inside the open hatchway and flicked some switches. Under the floor of the cockpit, beneath Marina's feet the engine throbbed.

'Do you know how to hold her into the wind while I winch up the anchor?' he asked her, and she nodded, stepping behind the wheel. He showed her where the gear levers were on the pedestal, then left her and went up on to the foredeck.

Under the palms of her hands the wood of the wheel was smooth and warm, turning easily when she corrected the swing of the yacht. Stainless steel fittings glittered in the sunlight, water slapped the sides of the hull and the small anchor winch creaked as Vittorio turned it.

Then suddenly the anchor was free and he was shouting to her to let the yacht drift backwards on the tide, away from the shore. Watching carefully, remembering all she had learned about seamanship from her father, Marina obeyed Vittorio's instructions. Slowly but inevitably the distance between the yacht and the pale rim of sand, the steep tree-covered slopes and the geranium-red roofs of the Villa Barberini increased. Vittorio came back to the cockpit and took the wheel from her. He pushed a gear lever and swung the wheel round. The yacht turned slowly until its bow pointed towards the gap between the two rocky headlands. The engine picked up speed, the bow lifted and the yacht surged towards the open sea.

CHAPTER FIVE

MARINA lay on the foredeck of the yacht with her back resting against a cushion which she had propped against one end of the cabin roof. Over her shirt she wore a thick white sweater that Vittorio had lent her because, offshore, the wind was cool, penetrating the thinness of her pink shirt. Beneath her the deck rolled first one way, then the other as the yacht plunged down between two waves and rose again on a sparkling crest. Spray flew past her in a swarm of tiny iridescent bubbles.

She tipped her head back and looked up to the top of the mainmast. Against the deep blue of the sky the mast gleamed yellow and the two sails, shimmering pale gold as they reflected the sun's light, curved to the breeze. The rigging whistled a wild tune and beneath the stem of the yacht as it forged through the water, the bow wave chuckled mischievously.

How long they had been sailing Marina did not know, nor did she care. Ever since Vittorio had ordered her to go to the dinghy she had had no control over where she went or what she did. He was in control as he steered his yacht through the blue and gold magic of the afternoon hours, taking her with him where he wished.

'She set her foot upon the ship,

No mariners could she behold,
But the sails were o' the taffeite
And the masts o' the beaten gold.'

The words of a poem she had read somewhere beat through her mind. Frowning, she withdrew her gaze from the go and the silky shimmering sails above and looked over her left shoulder, and surprise leapt through her so that she sat up straight and stared. The yacht was quite close to hand. A mountain loomed darkly against the sun-bright sky.

'Oh, hold your tongue of your weeping,' says he,
'Of your weeping now let it be;
'I will shew you how the lilies grow
'On the banks of Italy.'

More words of the poem danced through her mind. Where had she read it, and what was it about? Closing her eyes, she dredged the depths of her memory and suddenly saw quite clearly the poem printed on a page. The name of the poet and the title were printed after the last verse. It had been in a book of stories about the occult she had once read, and it had told the story of a woman who had gone sailing with the Devil, who had taken her to hell. The title was *The Daemon Lover*.

So that was where she had got the idea of Victor being her daemon lover, she thought, laughing a little to herself. How strange were the workings of the subconscious mind! The poem must have made a deep impression on her at the time she had read it during her vulnerable adolescence. Sensitive and imaginative, she had had a strong inclination to stories about the occult and witchcraft. When reading the poem she had probably identified with the woman in the story, so that when Vittorio, dark, foreign and satanic-looking, had appeared abruptly in her life and had arranged her visit to Biscari—not the banks of Italy but near enough to them—she had identified him with the daemon lover, the devil, who had taken possession of her soul, to torment and manipulate her, and even today had come unannounced, unexpectedly, to take control of her and carry her off to . . .?

She sat up sharply, shaking her head, and looked over her shoulder again. The hill was closer and the sun was behind it so that it looked dark and forbidding.

'O waten mountain is yon,' she said.
'All so dreary with frost and snow?'
'O yon is the mountain of hell,' he cried,
'Where you and I will go.'

Scrambling to her feet, Marina hurried along the side-deck to the cockpit, aware now that the engine was throbbing and that the sails, empty of wind, were shaking and that the yacht was entering a small almost landlocked bay, a pool of reflected golden light beyond which the land rose, shadowy and rocky.

'Where are we?' she asked as she stepped down into the cockpit.

'In Minore Bay at the northern end of Biscari,' he replied.

'Oh, thank goodness!' she whispered, and he gave her a surprised glance. 'I mean, I thought we were in. . . .' She broke off, rubbing a hand across her eyes, still confused by her memory of the strange poem, and her glance drifted stealthily to his feet. No, they weren't cloven. They looked quite normal in canvas sailing shoes. She looked up. Nor did he have horns. Those were coils of black hair, dishevelled by the wind that curved down over his broad brow. She was so relieved that he looked like a normal person that she smiled suddenly. He didn't smile back, but the expression in his eyes softened as their glance arrowed on her mouth.

'You were dreaming, perhaps,' he suggested softly. 'You must have been very tired, because you have slept nearly all the time we have been sailing.'

'Have I? How do you know?'

'Every time I went up on the foredeck to make sure you were still there and hadn't been swept overboard you were fast asleep,' he replied.

'Oh, I didn't know,' she said rather foolishly. But she remembered that when she had first gone to sit on the foredeck she had felt relaxed for the first time since she had come to Biscari. On this boat, in his company, she had felt, at last, at ease.

'Hold the wheel and keep the boat like this while I drop anchor,' he told her.

'We're going to anchor here?' she exclaimed, looking around the small bay. 'Why?'

'Because I would like to stop here for a while,' Vittorio replied coolly, and went up on to the deck before she had time to remonstrate further.

By the time the yacht was anchored, the engine turned off and the sails put away the sun was well down behind the shape of the island. No wind ruffled the surface of the gold-dappled water nor whispered in the trees on the shore. All was quiet and still. Entranced by the peaceful beauty of her surroundings, Marina sat in a corner of the cockpit watching the moon rise above the eastern horizon. From the cabin hatchway golden light streamed out. Vittorio was down there cooking. He had refused to let her help, had said she could only go down when the meal was ready.

She shouldn't really be there with him. It wasn't safe for them to be this close and alone: he had said so himself. Then why had he come to Biscari this afternoon? *'I'd no intention of coming,'* he had admitted. The wind had blown him. He had made it sound as if he had had no control over his own actions and behaviour.

He appeared in the hatchway.

'The food is ready now. Would you like to eat out there or in the cabin?' he asked.

'Out here,' she replied. Surely out here in the open they would be safe. Safe from whom? The question was mocking. Safe from each other, was the equally mocking answer.

There were flaps on the wheel pedestal which could be raised and propped up to make a small table. Vittorio put out circular table mats woven from straw, knives and forks, paper napkins and two wine glasses. Seated on opposite sides of the cockpit they ate grilled seafood, a mixture of prawns, tasty pieces of white fish and octopus served with rice, and drank a golden yellow semi-sweet wine that Vittorio said was called Albana and came from Italy.

Marina found herself doing most of the talking, answering his questions about her father's boat, telling of some of her sailing experiences. The sun went down, the sky darkened to a deep blue, the stars came out and the moon turned silver.

'It grows cool out here,' murmured Vittorio. 'Let's go into the cabin.'

He collected up their empty plates, picked up the wine bottle and stepped down into the hatchway. Marina picked up the two wine glasses and followed him.

Below decks the yacht was much bigger than any other she had ever been on. Near the companionway was the galley, L-shaped with a cooker, working surfaces and two small sinks. Beyond the galley the saloon was furnished with two long cushioned berths and a wide table. Shelves behind the berths were crammed with books and navigational aids. Through a narrow doorway she could see a passageway leading to the fore-cabin. Light was from two brass oil lamps mounted in gimbals on the bulkheads of the cabin.

'How long are we going to stay here?' asked Marina, sitting down on one of the berths, the one farthest from the table.

Vittorio looked up from pouring the rest of the wine into the two glasses.

'All night, if you wish,' he replied noncommittally.

'But what about. . . .' she began, then stopped. She wasn't really surprised by his answer.

'What about what?' he asked, his mouth quirking into the sudden wide white smile that transformed his face so quickly, giving a hint of a warm and generous personality which wasn't often on show. He came across to her and offered her one of the wine-glasses. She took it from him and he sat down beside her, flicking a switch of the radio that was set into the shelf behind him, and taped music, sweetly romantic, came softly through the speakers concealed in the corners of the cabin.

'Lucia might be worried when I don't turn up for dinner this evening. She'll wonder where I've gone,' Marina said, watching the play of light on the golden wine in her glass.

'No, she won't. Lucia knows you're with me.'

'Does Frankie?' she asked, looking at him sharply. His legs stretched before him, his head tilted back against the cushioned back of the berth, he was also studying the wine in his glass.

'Of course he does. I told Giulio to tell him you'd come sailing with me.'

'I see. I . . . I expect he's angry,' she murmured. She sipped some of her wine and glanced at him again. 'I think I should tell you. This morning Frankie asked me to marry him.'

'So?' he drawled. His eyes were half-closed as he continued to stare at his wine. 'And did you accept his proposal?'

'No, I didn't . . . well, not exactly. I said I would

only agree to marry him if he agreed to have another operation first.'

'And what did he say to that?'

'He accused me of blackmailing him, and he wanted to know who had put me up to it.'

Vittorio turned his head sharply to look at her, his eyes wide open, hard and bright, seeming to penetrate into her mind.

'Did someone put you up to it?' he asked.

'Yes, Giovanni did. Oh, you know very well he did,' she answered with a touch of irritation. 'You know too that was why Frankie was allowed to invite me to visit him. You knew when you came to London to find me what Giovanni had in mind, didn't you?'

He stared at her for a few moments, then began to laugh quietly.

'*Si*, I knew what Giovanni was going to suggest to you,' he replied, and raising his glass he drank all the wine that was in it and set the glass down on the shelf behind him. Changing his position, he sat sideways, raising one leg on to the berth so that his bent knee just touched her thigh. He stretched one arm along the top of the backrest behind her head. 'Did you tell Frankie that it was his grandfather's suggestion that you should use his proposal of marriage to manipulate him into having another operation?' he asked.

The soft sensuous glow was back in his eyes as they appraised her face and the deep, almost purring tone of his voice seemed to be totally unrelated to what he was actually saying. Behind her head his hand lifted. Gently his fingers began to play in her hair.

'No, I didn't,' she replied, looking down quickly, feeling colour rise in her cheeks. Never in all her life had she been with a man who could make love with his eyes and voice quite so blatantly while talking about something entirely different as Vittorio Matissi could. 'Bonnie came to play tennis then and he and she ... Oh, they're always fighting, those two ... and then she went off in a huff and he ... well, he asked me to marry him again.'

'Frankie was always stubborn,' he commented. 'What did you say to him? Did you give in and accept his proposal?'

'No. I realised then that if I stuck to my guns ... you know what I mean?' she asked, realising she was speaking very fast and might be using English idioms that were strange to him. He nodded, indicating that he understood, so she continued, 'It was possible that he might at least consider having another operation. So I said I would agree to marry him as soon as he came and told me he'd made the arrangements to have the operation.'

She raised her glass and drank the rest of the wine. Cool and sparkling, the liquid coursed down her throat. She lowered the glass and saw Vittorio's free hand reach out and take the empty glass from her to set it with the other glass on the shelf behind him. Realising that she was growing warm in the comfort of the cabin, Marina took off the thick sweater and he took that from her too, tossing it across the cabin on to the other berth.

Linking her fingers together on her knee, she stared at them, for some reason reluctant to look at Vittorio, afraid to meet his eyes again, trying to pretend she wasn't in the least affected by the feel of his fingers playing in her hair, the nudge of his knee against her thigh or the warm intimacy of his breath against her cheek when he spoke again.

'And did he agree to that?'

'More or less. He said he'd see Dr Spender this afternoon to find out how soon he could have the operation. He said as soon as he knew when Dr Spender could perform it he would then think about it and decide whether to go through with it or not. He became very arrogant and bossy and said I couldn't leave Biscari until he'd made up his mind. He also said that if he decided to have the operation I've to go with him to Switzerland and stay with him until he goes under the anaesthetic and be there when the operation is over.' She flicked a glance in the direction of the dark face now so near to her own face. 'That's why Giulio was appointed to be my bodyguard, I suppose,' she added. 'You know Frankie well. Do you think it will take him a long time to make up his mind one way or the other?'

The heavy lids dropped over his eyes. He seemed to be studying the shape of her mouth again instead of thinking of an answer to her question. And his fingers were no longer playing in her hair. They were stroking the nape of her neck, slowly and suggestively. Delicious tingles ran down her spine and a softness was spreading through the whole of her body. Under her blouse her breasts swelled and grew taut, straining against the fastenings of her blouse.

She swayed towards him involuntarily. The wine was singing in her head and all sensible coherent thought was being swamped by the flood of physical desire that was sweeping through her. Never had she wanted to be kissed so much; never had she wanted to be touched and fondled so much before.

'Vittorio,' she whispered, 'what do you think Frankie will decide to do?'

Vittorio's eyelids lifted and he looked right into her eyes. His own were very dark and had a glazed look about them. Marina wondered vaguely if he had heard what she had said.

'I think he'll decide to have the operation. Frankie wants you badly and he'll do anything to get what he wants,' he whispered, raising his other hand to touch her cheek.

'I had a feeling he might,' she muttered. 'Oh, dear, what shall I do? What shall I do?'

'Forget about Frankie for tonight and let's make the most of being here close together,' he replied.

But it's dangerous for us to be this close. The words were never spoken, although they rang through her head like a warning bell before desire drove out all reason. Intoxicated, not by the wine so much as by his nearness, by the scents of his sun-warmed skin and hair, by the titillating touch of his fingers, by the murmurous sound of his voice, Marina pressed her parted lips against his and lifting her hands buried her fingers deeply and greedily into the thick silkiness of his hair.

At the touch of her lips the passion he had been holding in while she had told him about Frankie's proposal exploded. His mouth dominated hers, lips pressing bruisingly, as he pushed her backwards on the berth. Oblivious to everything except the exciting sensations that close contact with him was arousing in her, Marina responded as best she could, sighing with delight when at last his warm fingers pushed aside her blouse and curved about her breast.

Somehow the blouse was removed, stroked away from her shoulders and slight but beautifully formed breasts. Somehow his shirt was gone too, revealing the taut smoothness of olive-tinted skin stretched across powerful muscles, the roughness of the black hair curling on his chest. Her hands learned about the smoothness and the roughness of his body while his lips explored her face, her throat, moving downwards, always downwards towards her breasts.

She moaned softly and deeply in her throat. Her body moved of its own accord, responding to the tender touch of his fingertips. She had no memory of anything that had gone before in her life. She knew only that it was for this that she had been created and now she was about to break out of the chrysalis which had been known as Marina Gregson until that moment, coolly beautiful but lacking in emotion, and she was to become at last a woman, throbbing with passion, designed to mate with this man for whom she had been subconsciously searching ever since she could

remember and who had come to her across the
sea.

Yet she didn't know him. Silent and dark, he
was like a deep pool, and if she plunged into that
pool she would go down and down for ever, never
finding the bottom of it, never really knowing him,
never being sure of him.

His hand slipped into the opening of her jeans,
fingers seeking to awaken dormant nerve endings,
and she gasped with pleasure, her fingernails
digging into his shoulders; and it was then it
awakened, quite suddenly, that deep-rooted,
primitive instinct to protect herself from his piracy.
She stiffened, her hands slid away from his back.
Her eyes opened and she saw the lamplight, the
dark face close to hers, the black hair coiling down
over the wide forehead.

'No,' she whispered. 'No, I can't. I can't!'

'*Si*, you can, *carissima*,' Vittorio whispered, and
his teeth glinted between his parted lips as he
smiled at her. 'I will show you how. We will take
our time, all night if necessary.'

Then his mouth smothered hers again in a kiss
that almost tamed her and again she felt his hand
moving over the curve of her hip down to her
thigh, and the protective instinct leapt into life
again. With her fists she struck at his shoulders.
His head lifted and he laughed at her, his eyes
dancing with devilry.

'So, you want to play rough games, eh?' he
mocked. 'I had not thought you would be like
that, but if it is what is needed to rouse you. . . .'

'No, oh, no!' she gasped, horrified at what he

was implying. 'I . . . I want you to stop.'

'Stop? Now? When we have come this far?' He was incredulous. 'You don't mean it!'

'Yes, I do. I do!'

Taking advantage of the slackness of his hold, she slid off the berth. Finding her blouse, she pulled it on quickly. She fastened her jeans and was beginning to button her blouse when Vittorio sprang suddenly to his feet, grasped her by the shoulders, his fingers biting cruelly into soft flesh. He jerked her towards him and her head snapped back. Fearfully she gazed up at the dark face poised above hers. It was distorted with fury and his eyes were blazing, and when his mouth covered hers again, his sharp teeth bit into the tender skin of her lips.

Panic-stricken now because she realised she had unwittingly offended his masculine pride by rejecting his lovemaking and he was going to use his superior physical strength to overwhelm her and take what he wanted, she hit at him again, her hands slapping sharply against the bare skin of his shoulders and against his head until suddenly he wrenched his mouth from hers and wrapping his arms around her held her tightly so that she couldn't move her arms any more; holding her, his head pressed hard against hers, until she stopped twisting and trying to escape and hung helplessly in his arms, sobbing for breath.

'Now perhaps you will tell me what that was all about, why you were fighting me,' he said quietly, relaxing his hold on her and pushing her away slightly so that he could look down into her face.

His eyes no longer blazed but were extremely dark and serious.

'I thought you were going to ... to. ...' Her voice quivered as a long shudder went through her and she shook her head from side to side, incapable of speech.

'You thought I was going to rape you,' he said for her, and she nodded mutely, avoiding his eyes.

His hands fell away from her waist where they had been resting lightly. She heard him mutter something in Italian below his breath, then he moved away from her. Looking up, Marina saw he had turned away from her and was pulling on his shirt. Relief washed through her because he had left her. Almost immediately the feeling was followed by another quite contrary feeling, one of disappointment because he had apparently decided not to force her to submit to his demands. Amazed and disgusted at herself for feeling that way, Marina sagged against the table which was behind her and clung to the edge of it with both hands. Tiny nerves which had been inflamed by his tantalising fingers were jumping agonisingly. It seemed that withdrawal was going to be very painful.

'I do not understand you.' Vittorio spoke in a low voice and she looked at him again. Facing her, he was buttoning his shirt and watching her from under frowning brows. 'Do you really believe I would have kissed you the way I did or that I would have touched you if you hadn't responded by kissing me and touching me? I believed you wanted me to do it.'

'I... I....', her throat was so dry her voice sounded like a creaky door hinge. She tried to clear it and went on hoarsely, 'When we kissed first I did want you to ... and I wanted to ... but then I remembered,' she said lamely.

'You remembered what?' His shirt fastened, he was standing with his arms folded across his chest and his face was set in hard lines. No longer her daemon lover, he looked now like a stern judge about to pass sentence upon her for wrongdoing.

'I remembered the other women and I decided I'd no wish to be numbered among your amorous conquests,' she explained, lifting her head proudly, challenging him across the space between them.

'My *what*?' Vittorio exclaimed, incredulous laughter rumbling in his voice and breaking up the stern lines of his face. '*Non capisco*—I don't understand. Please explain.'

'I was referring to the women you've ... you've seduced,' she whispered. 'I've no wish to join their numbers.'

'I see.' Laughter still quivered in his voice, but his face was darkening, slowly growing grim again as he advanced towards her. 'And who told you about those other women?' he asked, his voice silky with menace.

'Frankie,' Marina admitted nervously, her hands gripping the edge of the table even more tightly when she saw anger glint wickedly in his eyes again. 'I'm not like them,' she added defensively.

'No?' His eyebrows tilted derisʲ/ely and his

glance swept over her insolently. 'What makes you so different from them?'

'I . . . I can't make love, just for kicks, for fun,' she whispered. 'I can't make love with someone who doesn't love me. And you don't love me.'

In the silence that followed she heard a halliard slap against the mast, the anchor chain creak, the rigging whine as the boat swung to face the rising night wind. She also heard Vittorio's exasperated intake of breath.

'I still don't understand what you mean when you talk of love,' he said. 'But I do know when I'm attracted to a woman. I know when I want to make love to her because I feel it here.' He hit his fist against the lower part of his stomach.

Her eyes flew up to his face. His burning glance made her nerves leap. If she could have stepped back from him she would have done.

'I've thought about you day and night, ever since I met you in London,' he continued softly. 'Much against my will I've thought about you all this past week. That is why I let the wind blow me today to Biscari. I wanted to see you again to find out if I would still want to make love to you when I was face to face with you.' He drew in another hissing breath. 'I met you on the beach and I wanted you, so I asked you to come sailing with me. Oh, yes, I had every intention of seducing you, but only because I believe you felt the same as I did.' He stepped close to her, his breath fanning her cheek. 'Can you deny, Marina, that you've felt the same as I have? Haven't you lain awake at night wishing you were with me, wishing we were close like this, wishing I was touching you?' His fingers stroked her cheek and slid under her chin as if he would raise her face to receive his kiss. 'Isn't that why you came to meet me today? Why you came sailing with me?'

Jerking her head sideways so that his fingers fell away from her chin, Marina shook it from side to side.

'No, I can't deny it,' she whispered.

'Then for God's sake why are you resisting this dangerous compulsion both of us have to make love to each other?' he demanded harshly, thrusting his hands into his jeans pockets as if he didn't trust them. 'Why are you being so cruel to yourself and to me?'

'Because . . . because . . . Oh, I'm sorry, I didn't mean to be cruel. Oh, don't look at me like that.' She shaded her eyes with one hand as if shading them from a blinding light. 'I shouldn't have come and you shouldn't have asked me to come. We both knew it would be dangerous if we got too close to each other.' She drew a sobbing breath. 'Please try to understand that for me physical attraction isn't enough. There has to be some sort of commitment before I can make love. If . . . If I stay the night with you and let you make love to me I'll lose my self-respect and afterwards I'd feel I'd been used, cheapened.'

She flicked a glance at his face. It looked as if it had been carved in stone. Only the eyes were alive, and they were blazing with anger. Again she wished she could have stepped away from him, but it wasn't necessary for her to move. Vittorio moved instead, turning sharply away. From the hanging locker he took down his sailing jacket and shrugged into it. On his way to the companionway he looked back at her.

'This time it is you who has made the mistake,' he said coldly and flatly. 'We won't stay here for the night after all. We'll go back now and you can return to the Barberini web. Presumably you feel safer there than you do with me.'

Almost two hours later from the corner of the cockpit seat where she sat with her feet on the seat, her knees bent up and her arms curled about them, Marina saw the lights of the Villa Barberini shining out from the dark hillside above the small horseshoe-shaped bay. She saw them with a sense of relief because at last the short voyage from Minore Bay was ending. Sailing by moonlight with a fresh breeze filling the shimmering silvered sails as the yacht bounded over dark blue, silver-laced waves should have been romantic, but in reality it had been torture. Miserable and silent, she had crouched, wishing she had been able to blot from her mind all that had happened between Vittorio and herself in the lamplit cabin. But it was as if her mind had become a television screen on which the same programme was being repeated over and over again.

If only Vittorio would speak to her! She glanced sideways at him. He was a dark figure behind the wheel. Dark and silent, he was still the mysterious stranger, the daemon lover, tempting her to abandon the principles she had held for years, and about whom she knew very little for all she had been close to him; for all she had kissed him and had touched him intimately.

Oh, God! Desire knifed through her and her head went down on her knees. Why had she resisted his lovemaking? It wasn't the first time she had expected too much from a man. But what was it she had expected from Vittorio? A declaration of his undying love for her? A proposal of marriage perhaps before she would let him make love to her?

Her body swayed with the motion of the boat, the movement seeming to express the swaying of her emotions, first one way and then the other; swaying between relief because he hadn't forced her to stay the night with him and regret because she hadn't had the courage to go all the way with him.

Through the mist of her misery she heard him speak at last, and raised her head. She felt sodden, as if she had been weeping for hours, and yet her eyes were dry.

'What?' she mumbled.

'We have arrived. Hold the wheel, *per favore.*' He was cool and crisp, autocratic. 'I'll drop the anchor.'

Empty of wind, the sails shook as the bow of the boat pointed into the faint breeze from the shore. Moving lethargically, Marina took Vittorio's place at the wheel and he went forward.

The anchor was dropped, the sails were lowered. Vittorio pulled the dinghy alongside and she stepped down into it and sat on the stern thwart. He joined her and began to row to the shore. In a few minutes they were there and she was stepping out on the beach, more or less opposite the place where the steps came down from the villa.

She began to walk towards the step, then realised he wasn't with her. She turned back.

'Aren't you coming to ... to see Lucia?' she asked.

'No. You can tell her I've decided to go back to Catania tonight,' he replied. He began to push the dinghy into the water.

'Thank you for taking me sailing,' Marina muttered stiffly. 'Your boat ... *Nesaea* ... is beautiful. I'm glad I've seen her and sailed on her. I wish. ...' She broke off as alarmingly tears were filling her eyes at the thought of parting from him, realising that if she had stayed with him she could have gone to Catania too. She could have escaped from the Barberini web.

'What do you wish?' he asked softly, turning to her.

'That it ... I mean that I could have behaved differently,' she whispered, peering up at him, trying to read the expression on his face but seeing only the glint of his eyes in the moonlight, the sheen of skin stretched tight over prominent bones.

'It's a little late in the day for you to be wishing that,' he said dryly. 'I could say I wish that we had never met, but it's too late for that too. Too late for regrets, Marina. The damage has been done. I'll leave you now. *Buona sera*.'

He pushed the dinghy off again, leapt aboard it and began to row. Soon she couldn't see him or the dinghy any more because both had become a part of the pattern of light and dark on the moving water.

'*Buona sera, signorina.*' The voice spoke behind her, startling her, and she whirled round. Giulio, his white shirt gleaming in the moonlight, was standing there. 'Was the sailing good?' he enquired.

'*Si, si, grazie.* The sailing was good,' she gasped, her hand going to her breast as if to still the sudden swift beat of her heart. Her fingers curled against the feel of soft wool beneath her. She was still wearing Vittorio's sweater. 'How long have you been waiting here?' she asked.

'Since you left with Signor Matissi. Signor Barberini said I was to wait and watch for your return. You go up now, to the villa?'

'Yes, yes, of course. It must be late.'

'It is ten-thirty, *signorina.*' They walked across the beach, their feet sinking into the soft sand. The wind whispered sadly in the pines that arched over the long flight of shallow steps.

'I'm sorry you had to wait so long,' Marina apologised, taking one last look at the bay before she started to go up the steps. Faintly she heard the throb of an engine and thought she saw the glimmer of a white sail in the moonlight as it was hoisted up a mast.

'*No importa,*' replied Giulio cheerfully. 'It is my job to wait and watch. Signor Barberini said I was to take you to him as soon as you came back. I think we will find him in the hallway.'

After the moonlit darkness outside the interior of the house seemed very bright. The mosaic tiles of the entrance hall gleamed blue, green and white and the coverings of the Romanesque sofas shone softly yellow. Not only Frankie was in the hall; Lucia was there too, and Giovanni, the Spenders and Emilia. They were talking, but stopped when they saw her approaching. Frankie swished up to her. There was a hostile glint in his eyes.

'So you come back at last,' he said.

'Ah, how you are pale!' Lucia came forward anxiously exuding motherly concern. 'I hope you did not have the seasickness—the waves, they were rough, eh?' She made a swooping action with one hand.

'No, I wasn't sick,' replied Marina, rubbing her cheeks hoping to instil some colour in them. 'I'm sorry I missed dinner. We anchored in a bay at the north of the island. In Minore Bay. Do you know it? We had dinner there.'

'I know it,' said Emilia, nodding. 'Vittorio and I used to sail there often when we were younger,' she explained to Howard Spender, next to whom she was sitting.

'Come, sit down,' said Lucia, taking Marina's hand and leading her over to another sofa. 'I am very glad you have come back safely. I worry when you go with Vittorio. Sometimes he is . . . ah, I do not know how to say it in English.'

'He is a selfish, inconsiderate swine,' said Frankie between his teeth as he brought his chair to a stop close to Marina. He snatched her hand from her knee and held it possessively between both of his. 'And he guessed I would be furious if he took you sailing with him. Why did you go?

Did he force you to go?'

'No, no, I went because I wanted to go. I like sailing and I wanted to see his boat,' she replied.

'But you promised you would stay with me,' he retorted. 'You're not going anywhere with him again—I won't let you. You see, I've made up my mind, Marina. I've decided to have the operation.' He leaned towards her and whispered, 'Now the ball is in your court, so what are you going to do about it?' He swung his chair around suddenly so that he was facing the others and said loudly, 'Listen, everybody! I've got an announcement to make. This morning I asked Marina to marry me. She said she would only agree to marry me if I agreed first to have another operation. It's been hard for me to make up my mind, but I ... I've just decided that I will have the operation—on one condition,' he turned his head and gave Marina a bright malicious glance. 'I'll have the operation as soon as Howard can perform it if ... and only if ... Marina consents to become engaged to me now ... while you're all here. Marina,' he tugged at her hand, 'what do you say? Do you consent? Will you marry me when the operation is over?'

Marina looked around her at the others. Beside her Lucia was murmuring softly in Italian, something that sounded like a prayer. Beyond her Emilia was smiling, a faint knowledgeable smile, as she stared across the hall at something Marina couldn't see. Bonnie suddenly jumped to her feet and walked away, disappearing into the shadows under one of the archways. Howard Spender, looking thoroughly relaxed, was puffing at a cigar and gazing up at the ceiling as if he was admiring the design of it.

And Giovanni, the squat black spider sitting in the corner of his web, was looking right at her, his dark eyes unwinking, one hand holding his cigar near his mouth as if he were about to take a puff at it. Slowly, almost imperceptibly, he nodded at her. Marina swallowed hard and licked her dry lips. They tasted of salt spray, reminding her of where she had been that afternoon and with whom she had been. Oh, why hadn't she stayed with Vittorio for the night? Why hadn't she asked him to take her to Catania with him?

'*Ave Maria,*' Lucia muttered.

'Marina, you promised, you promised!' Frankie's voice was rising excitedly. The pressure was on; the gossamer threads of the web were tightening around her. She squeezed Frankie's hand reassuringly, forced herself to smile.

'I'm glad, so very glad you've decided to have the operation,' she said.

'But only if you say yes, you'll marry me,' he insisted. 'You have to promise you'll marry me after it is over first. I won't have it done until you agree to marry me.'

Again she glanced quickly at Giovanni. Again he nodded.

'Yes, I promise to marry you after the operation is over,' she whispered, looking straight at Frankie. Triumph glittered in his eyes before they were hidden as he bent his head to kiss the back of her hand.

'And so at last we are engaged,' he announced. 'And next week I will go to Switzerland to have the operation.'

'*Grazie, grazie!*' Lucia repeated the word over and over again and flinging her arms about Marina kissed her affectionately on both cheeks.

'Lucia is saying that you have made her very happy and she is glad you came here,' Emilia translated, coming across and offering a slim hand to Marina. 'May I congratulate you,' she added, a slight mocking smile curving her lips. She leaned forward and said in a low voice, 'You've played your cards very well. It was clever of you to go off with Vittorio for a few hours, just what was needed to tip Frankie over into making a decision. He's been simmering with jealousy ever since you went sailing.' Emilia's smile became rather taut and false. 'And so have I,' she added. She glanced towards the archway where Giulio lounged. 'Where is Vittorio now? Didn't he come up to the house with you?'

'No. He's gone back to Catania,' replied Marina, and Emilia immediately turned away to tell Lucia and Frankie, while Bonnie slid on to the sofa beside Marina.

'I'm glad too that Frankie's decided to have the operation at last, but I can't say I'm glad he's going to marry you because it wouldn't be true,' the American girl whispered. Then suddenly she hugged Marina, kissed her cheek and murmured, 'What's the matter? You look awful.'

'Emilia thinks I went with Vittorio deliberately,

to make Frankie jealous so he would make up his mind,' said Marina.

'And didn't you?'

'No, of course I didn't. I'd never think of doing anything like that.'

'Then why did you go with Vittorio?' Bonnie's eyes were bright and curious. 'Have you fallen for him? Lots of women do, so I hear. Oh, Marina, what a triangle it would be—you married to Frankie and having an affair with his uncle on the side!' she exclaimed.

'Shush!' said Marina warningly. 'Don't say that. Nothing like that is going to happen. . . .'

'Marina,' Giovanni spoke quietly but imperiously and she looked across at him. 'Come here, *per favore*,' he said.

'Excuse me,' she said to Bonnie and went across to sit beside the old man.

'You have done well, *signorina*,' he complimented her. 'I am pleased. There were times during this week when I thought we were going to have to wait a long time for him to propose to you, but I should have guessed that a woman like you would know intuitively how to handle a jealous, possessive person like Francesco.' He studied the ring of thick ash which had formed at one end of his cigar. 'It was a brilliant move on your part to go off with Vittorio this afternoon,' he went on softly. 'I couldn't have thought of a better move myself.'

'But I didn't go. . . .' began Marina, who was beginning to feel a little sick, only to break off when Giovanni held up his hand.

'Never admit there was no purpose in what you

did,' he told her. 'And now we must make arrangements for you to go with Francesco and hs mother to the clinic in Switzerland. Dr Spender will be leaving tomorrow to make preparations and he suggested that Francesco should travel on Monday and enter the clinic that evening to be settled into his room. On Tuesday he will have the usual preliminary tests and if everything is correct the operation will take place on Wednesday. We should know by the end of the week if the operation has been successful and if Francesco is able to walk again.'

'What are you saying to her, Grandfather?' demanded Frankie jealously, as he swished up to them in his chair. 'Why are you whispering to Marina?'

'I am welcoming her to our family,' Giovanni said blandly. 'Isn't that what you've been wanting me to do for some time?'

'Then can we announce our engagement officially tomorrow?' asked Frankie, grinning happily. 'I want everyone to know. I want the whole world to know.'

'Not yet,' said Giovanni, still smooth. 'I think it best if the engagement is not made public until after the operation.'

'But we can make it known to members of the family, can't we?' said Frankie, his lips pouting sulkily. 'I do so want Vittorio to know.'

'You can be sure Lucia will inform her family as soon as she can get to a telephone,' said Giovanni dryly, then added something in Italian as Lucia, carrying a silver tray on which there were crystal glasses full of champagne, approached them.

As she took one of the glasses Marina forced herself to smile and to look relatively happy as a newly-engaged woman should look, and when Giovanni made a toast to the success of Frankie's operation and to his future happiness she chinked her glass against Frankie's and drank.

What else could she do? She was well and truly caught in the Barberini web, and for the moment she could see no way of escape.

CHAPTER SIX

FROM the balcony of her bedroom in a luxurious hotel overlooking the eastern end of Lake Geneva Marina watched the mists of morning draw back from the south-eastern shore to unveil the sturdy stone walls, the sloping slate roofs of the medieval castle of Chillon which was situated on a small island close to the shores of the lake. Behind the castle the slopes of a high mountain, darkly silhouetted against the pale morning sky, rose upwards. It guarded the entrance to the Rhône Valley and beyond its darkness other mountains, the serrated snow-crowned peaks of the Dents du Midi, shimmered like silver in the spring sunlight.

Ten days had passed since Frankie had decided to have the operation on the lower part of his spine to release the pinched nerves that had prevented him from walking. Once he had made the decision the Barberini organisation had swung into action and had transported him, Marina and Lucia from Biscari to Switzerland. First they had been whisked by helicopter to Catania airport and from there they had flown in Giovanni's private jet plane to Geneva.

From Geneva they had been driven in a hired limousine along the northern side of the lake to the private orthopaedic clinic at which Howard Spender was one of a group of famous consultant surgeons. Frankie had been settled into a room there and Marina and Lucia had been brought to this hotel, set in beautiful landscaped gardens not far from the town of Montreux, and had been installed in an elegant suite of rooms on the second floor.

The day after he had arrived at the clinic Frankie had undergone all the usual pre-operative tests to make sure that he had been healthy enough to receive surgical treatment. All the tests had been positive and the operation had been performed the next day. As she had promised him, Marina had stayed with him until he had been given the anaesthetic, holding his hand as he had requested until he had lost consciousness. Lucia had been present too.

The operation had been done and had been pronounced successful by Dr Spender. As soon as they were allowed Marina and Lucia had visited Frankie in the clinic and they had gone every day since. Frankie was responding well to physiotherapy and was already on his feet and walking about with the aid of a *zimmer*. Last night he had talked to Marina about making their engagement official and had wanted to set the date of their marriage. She had told him that she couldn't marry him after all, but he had refused to believe her.

'But we are engaged to be married!' he had exclaimed angrily.

'The engagement isn't official,' she had argued. 'Frankie, please try to understand. I agreed to become engaged to you to help you. Your grandfather asked me to. He thought it would be a good way to get you to have the operation.'

'So I was right—you were put up to it,' he had said, his lips thinning against his teeth, and he had muttered something virulent in Italian. His hand had shot out and he had grasped her wrist. 'But you're caught now,' he had muttered between his teeth, 'and I'm not going to let you go. We're going to be married and I'm not going to wait until we return to Biscari. I'm going to beat Grandfather at his own game. We'll be married here by special licence before I leave the clinic.'

'No, no!' She had sprung to her feet. 'I won't marry you, I won't. I can't!'

She had run from his room, almost colliding with a nurse who had been about to enter and had gone to find Lucia who had been closeted with Howard Spender getting information about Frankie's condition. They had returned to the hotel and Marina had spent a restless night wondering how to cross the bridge that Giovanni had suggested she didn't cross before she reached it and which now loomed before her; wondering how to escape from the web which she herself had helped Giovanni and Frankie to spin around her.

She still had a strong feeling that Giovanni didn't want Frankie to marry her, and that was why he had insisted that the engagement shouldn't be made official until after the operation had been proved successful and Frankie was walking properly. The wily old man had left room for manoeuvre and because no announcement had been made publicly, because no engagement ring had been given, she wouldn't feel honour bound to marry Frankie.

But Frankie was making it so difficult for her to leave him. Giulio had travelled north with them, and everywhere she went he went with her. She had hoped that perhaps Giovanni himself might have taken some action to help her to leave, but so far nothing had happened. He was still on Biscari, and apart from the message of congratulations he had sent to Frankie on the success of the operation nothing had been heard from him.

If only she had stayed last Saturday night with Vittorio on his yacht she might not be here now, trying to disentangle herself from the unofficial engagement. If she had stayed with Vittorio he might have taken her to Catania with him and by now she might have been back in London. Or . . . a quiver of excitement tingled through her . . . she might have agreed to become his mistress.

Have you fallen for him? Lots of women do, so I hear. Oh, Marina, what a triangle it would be if you married Frankie and had an affair with his uncle! Bonnie Spender's remarks had haunted her all week, showing her clearly what the future would be like if she did marry Frankie. Attracted to Vittorio as she was she would be for ever fighting the temptation to be with him whenever he visited his nephew. She had fallen for him. Night and day she thought about him, wishing she had had the opportunity to know him better, wishing, above all, she had stayed the night with him on his yacht; wishing she hadn't repulsed him.

Too late for regrets. The damage has been done. Vittorio's words, and they too had haunted her as she had recognised how true they were. No, she couldn't marry Frankie and risk meeting Vittorio regularly. She wouldn't be able to stand the strain of being married to one man while she was in love with another. She had to escape somehow. If only she could give Giulio and Lucia the slip and go by train to France! Switzerland had an excellent train service and she knew that if she could get to Basel she would be able to catch an express that went right through France as far as Calais, thence to England. But even if she could only get to Paris, that would be far enough. Once there she could go and see Marius and perhaps persuade him to give her a job.

'Marina?' From the room behind her Lucia called. No doubt she was ready to go for the daily visit to the clinic to see how Frankie was progressing. Marina didn't want to go. After last night's argument she didn't want to face Frankie again, afraid that he might have done something about getting a special licence. She wondered if she could plead having a headache or sickness of some sort to get out of going and, once Lucia had departed for the clinic, find some way of dodging Giulio.

She stepped through the open French window into the pleasant pink and white room. Dressed in her customary black with touches of white at the throat and wrists, Lucia was standing just inside the open door that led to the sitting room of the suite. Her dark eyes were twinkling with good humour and her broad generous lips were curved into a pleased smile.

'Come into the sitting room, *per favore*,' she said. 'We have a visitor.'

'Oh. Who?' asked Marina, hoping that Giovanni had come at last.

'Come and see,' replied Lucia teasingly, and went back into the other room.

Marina glanced quickly at her reflection in a long mirror and, satisfied that she looked presentable in the skirt of her grey gaberdine suit and a blouse made from silk striped in grey, blue and pink which had a high frilled neckline tied with a thin grey ribbon, she walked across into the other room.

A man was standing at one of the windows of the room looking out at the view, his dark figure silhouetted against the sunlight outside; a man with wide shoulders and black hair that waved down the back of his head and clustered in curls at his nape. He was dressed casually in beige pants and a dark brown suede golf jacket.

Marina's breath caught in her throat and she stopped in her tracks, her hand going to the frilled neckline of her blouse as if she found it suddenly too tight. She stared at the man as if she couldn't believe her eyes, blinked and looked at Lucia, then looked back towards the window. He was still there.

'Vittorio, Marina is here. Please to say good morning to her,' said Lucia, who was sitting on a brocade love seat and looking very pleased still.

Vittorio half turned away from the window. From under down-drooping black lashes his dark eyes appraised Marina, but he didn't smile at her.

'Hello. How are you?' he asked coolly.

'Very well, thank you,' she replied stiffly, wishing she could have controlled the rush of colour to her face in the same way she could control her voice. She walked over to Lucia and sat down beside her. 'When did you come?' she asked politely. Oh, how difficult it was to pretend to be cool and calm when every impulse was urging her to show her delight at seeing him again.

'Yesterday, to Geneva. I had business there. This morning I drove here to see Frankie, and of course Lucia and yourself. It seems Frankie is making good progress.'

He spoke stiltedly and his accent was more pronounced than usual, and he avoided looking directly at her.

'I am trying to persuade Vittorio to stay until Friday, then he can escort us back to Biscari,' Lucia explained slowly to Marina. During the past ten days while they had been staying in the hotel her English had improved considerably. Every day Marina had insisted that they held conversations over meals in English or in Italian so that they could both learn not only how to speak another language but also more about each other. The experiment had paid off and they were both understanding each other much better.

'I can't stay until Friday,' Vittorio said flatly.

Immediately Lucia abandoned her attempts to speak in English and spoke to him in Italian, words pouring out of her as she tried to persuade him to do what she asked. He shrugged his shoulders indifferently, turning away to look out of the window again, and Lucia said to Marina,

'Usually he help me. He is the best of brothers and sons. Always he has helped me, my sisters and our mother. When Papa died and there was no money Vittorio gave up his studies to be an architect to return to Catania and build the business up again so that my mother would not be poor and so that my sisters would have education and marry well. And since Raimondo, my husband, died, Vittorio has helped me with Francesco, has been like a father to him. If it wasn't for Vittorio going to London to find you. . . .'

'You talk too much, Lucia.' Vittorio swung round from the window to glare impatiently at his sister.

'I do not think so,' Lucia retorted. 'All this week Marina and I talk to each other. We learn much about each other, and I want her to know about you, how kind and generous you can be and how she can depend on you. When she is married to Francesco you will be her uncle as well as his. Have you thought of that?'

'I have thought of it,' replied Vittorio tautly. 'It

isn't a relationship I enjoy, being an uncle,' he added, his lips twisting cynically. 'And I already have two nieces.'

'My sisters Maria and Caterina both have daughters,' Lucia explained, smiling at Marina. 'And now Vittorio tells me there is to be another wedding in the family beside yours and Francesco's. Our youngest sister Teresa has announced her engagement.' She looked at Vittorio. 'Once she is married and off your hands you can start planning for yourself, Vittorio. It is time you married too.'

'So you are always saying,' he retorted. He glanced at Marina. 'Have you and Frankie set the date for your wedding yet?'

'I ... we ... I ....' she stammered, and was immediately interrupted by Lucia.

'No, not yet. Not until we all return to Biscari,' Lucia said positively. 'Then the date will be announced and we will have a big engagement party and everyone will come to it. You will bring Mamma, Vittorio, and Teresa will bring her fiancé. And Maria and Caterina will bring their husbands and children. And I have talked to Sophia by phone. She and Severo will come too.'

'And will Emilia bring her husband and their children?' asked Vittorio mockingly.

'No, I do not think so,' sighed Lucia, her mood changing mercurially, her plump face expressing sadness, and becoming tired of trying to express herself in English she went off into a flurry of Italian, obviously explaining something about Emilia and her husband. Then she turned to

Marina and said apologetically, 'Excuse me, please, Marina. I cannot say it in English well—I do not know the words. Emilia is upset because her husband is no good any more. He cannot do it.'

Marina flashed a quick glance at Vittorio as she tried to control an impulse to laugh outright at Lucia's innocently phrased remarks. His eyes met hers briefly. Amusement glinted in them and the muscle at one corner of his mouth quivered as if he too was having difficulty in controlling his mirth. Then the moment of shared amusement was over because Lucia spoke again.

'Emilia try to get a divorce and then Vittorio can marry her at last.'

'*Stai quieta*, Lucia! You don't know what you're talking about,' said Vittorio sharply, and continued to berate his sister in Italian, calling her an interfering gossip. Lucia, taking offence at what he was saying, got to her feet and after spitting some words at him, said to Marina, with great dignity,

'It is time we go to visit Francesco. Are you ready?'

'Not quite. I'll go and fetch my jacket and handbag,' said Marina, and returned to her bedroom.

It was when she was slipping on her suit jacket that she remembered her plan to plead feeling not well so that she wouldn't have to go with Lucia to the clinic. But now Vittorio had come she wondered how she could contrive to speak to him alone to ask him to help her get away to France. After all, he had told her once that he was the only person who could help her if the situation became too difficult for her to handle.

When she went back to the sitting room he was there, alone, lounging in an armchair looking through one of Lucia's magazines. He didn't look up or acknowledge the fact that she had come back into the room and, thinking that Lucia was still getting ready to go out, Marina sat down on the love-seat again and searched her mind for ways of asking him to help her.

From under her lashes she studied his face. In contrast to the cream-coloured turtle-necked sweater of fine ribbed wool that he was wearing under the suede jacket his face looked dark and forbidding. Her initial excitement on seeing him so unexpectedly had faded now and had been replaced by a feeling of shyness. There was so much she wanted to say to him, but his cool attitude towards her, apart from that one warm moment of shared amusement, pushed her away. He seemed as inaccessible to her as one of the high mountain peaks she could see through the window, and she wondered how she could ever have thought of asking him to help her.

Suddenly he tossed the magazine aside and looked straight at her.

'Lucia has gone to the clinic,' he said abruptly.

'Oh.' She was surprised. 'Why has she gone without me?'

'Because I told her to.' His eyes narrowed slightly as he stared at her. 'I wanted to talk to you without her being around listening and butting in,' he added curtly.

'Did Signor Barberini ask you to come here?' she asked hopefully.

'He knew I was coming to Geneva,' he replied, evasively she thought. His gaze seemed to become more intent. 'Are you really going to marry Frankie?' he asked.

'Are you really going to marry Emilia when she has divorced her husband?' Marina retorted.

'Now why the hell should you concern yourself with that?' he queried softly, leaning forward to stare at her even more closely.

'I could say the same to you,' she said defensively. 'Why should you concern yourself with my affair with Frankie?'

Slowly he leaned back in the chair again, his lips curving into their slightly mocking smile, his lashes hiding his expression.

'Because, as the uncle who has been acting as a father to him, I wouldn't like to see him married for his money,' he drawled provocatively.

'I'm not marrying Frankie for his money!' she snapped angrily, glaring at him, and when his smile widened into a grin she added exasperatedly, 'Oh, you know why I agreed to marry him!'

'Do I?' Vittorio raised his eyebrows.

'I told you, when I went sailing with you. I told you I'd promised to marry him if he agreed to have another operation. Don't you remember?'

'I remember everything about our voyage together,' he replied, his grin fading as his suddenly hot glance roved suggestively over her.

'And I haven't forgiven you yet for refusing to stay the night with me.'

Marina felt hot colour rush into her cheeks again. Avoiding his glance, she looked down at her thin envelope handbag which was resting on her knees and played with the flap.

'Frankie was very upset because I'd gone sailing with you,' she muttered. 'Did you know he would be? Was that why you invited me to go with you, to make him jealous?' She looked up suddenly and challengingly.

'Did you go sailing with me to make him jealous so that he would be pushed into making a decision?' he countered, his eyes narrowing to dark slits, his lips curling cynically, and she guessed he had seen Emilia during the past week and that the woman had told him of her suspicions.

'No, I didn't. I went with him because I wanted to see your boat and I wanted to go sailing with you,' she replied in a low voice. 'But when I got back to the villa Frankie decided there and then, in front of everyone—his grandfather, his mother, Emilia, Dr Spender and Bonnie—that he would have the operation, but only if I would keep my promise to agree to marry him.'

'And so you were well and truly trapped in the Barberini web, as I had warned you you would be,' Vittorio said dryly.

'Oh, I should have guessed you'd be delighted to say "I told you so"!' exclaimed Marina, and springing to her feet she walked over to the window so that she wouldn't have to face his mocking gaze. 'I had to agree to marry him when

he said he'd have the operation,' she went on. 'I'd
promised him I would. And I don't break promises
. . . at least, not unless there's a good reason for
breaking them. And it worked. The operation has
been done and he's beginning to walk again.' She
paused, then when he didn't say anything she
added, 'And now I don't know what to do.'

She didn't hear him move and didn't know he
was behind her until he spoke quietly, his breath
fluffing the hair over her right ear.

'Don't you want to marry him?' he said.

She shook her head from side to side, her fine
blonde hair flirting out.

'No, I don't. I've never wanted to marry him. I
only said I would to get him to have the operation,
to help him,' she whispered. 'Last night I told him
I couldn't marry him, but he wouldn't believe me,
and he said he's going to get a special licence and
marry me in the clinic before we leave Biscari.
Somehow I have to get away . . . today!'

'Then why don't you leave, now?'

She turned to face him, searching his face. As
usual it was impassive, giving no hint of his real
feelings, and his eyes were opaque, wells of
darkness not even reflecting her image.

'I've thought of that, but it isn't possible. Giulio
is here watching everything I do and going
everywhere I go.' She pointed to the main door of
the suite. 'He's out there now waiting for me to go
to the clinic. And when I go he'll go with me.'

They were standing very close to each other as
they had stood when they had met on the beach at
Biscari, and Vittorio was looking at her as he had

looked at her then. He wanted her, and without saying anything, without touching her, he was telling her that he did just by looking at her.

'You're quite sure you want to leave?' he asked softly.

'Quite sure.'

'There would be no coming back if you do leave.'

'I wouldn't want to come back. I've done what I said I would do to help Frankie and now I want to leave to get on with my own life.' Marina looked at him pleadingly. 'You said once that you're the only person who could or would help me if I couldn't handle the situation. Could you, would you help me now to get to France? I have enough money to pay the train fare to Paris and I think I can get a job there.'

His eyebrows slanted together in a quick frown and his mouth hardened.

'With whom?' he demanded.

'Marius Gaudin, the fashion designer.'

His frown deepened and thrusting his hands into his trouser pockets he swung away from her to pace across the room. Uneasily aware that she had said something to annoy him, Marina watched him while she chewed at her lower lip wondering what she would do if he refused to help her. At last he came back to her to stand in front of her, but not as close as he had been.

'I'll help you, but only if you agree to do exactly as I tell you,' he told her.

'More blackmail?' she challenged him, tilting her chin at him.

'If you like to call it that,' he replied, shrugging indifferently.

'What do you want me to do?'

'First of all I'd like you to write a note to Lucia. If you leave now without telling her where you've gone she will worry unnecessarily and will go and upset Frankie, and he'll have the whole Swiss police force out looking for you. In the note you will tell Lucia you've gone out with me for a drive into the mountains. She'll do and say nothing if she knows you're with me, and that will give you time to get away. When you've written the note, pack your cases and come down to the front entrance of the hotel in about half an hour. I'll be waiting for you there.'

'But what about Giulio?'

'I'm going to deal with him now,' he said. 'Will you do what I suggest?'

'Yes, if you'll help me to get away.'

'You can be sure I will,' Vittorio replied rather grimly. 'You see, like Giovanni, I don't want Frankie to marry you and I'll do anything to help you get away from him.'

Abruptly he turned away and strode over to the door of the suite. He left the room without looking back. The door closed quietly behind him.

Marina didn't hesitate. At the writing desk she took out a sheet of the thick hotel paper and wrote to Lucia. She put only,

'I have gone for a drive with Vittorio. Do not worry, Marina.'

She put the paper in an envelope which she addressed to Signorina Barberini and left it on top of the desk. In the bedroom she packed quickly and methodically, then carried her cases to the outer door of the room. Cautiously she opened it and looked out. The flower-scented, luxuriously carpeted corridor was empty. Giulio was not there. Picking up her cases, Marina left the room and walked along to the elevator. In a few minutes Vitterio was taking the cases from her and they were going through the revolving doors out into the crisp morning air. The sunshine was bright, glittering on the windows, and the chromium of the car which was parked in front of the hotel.

'Get in,' ordered Vittorio, and carried her cases round to the back of the car to put them in the boot.

'I . . . I thought I'd take a taxi,' she said, trying to assert control over her own actions again.

'This is a rented car,' he replied coolly. 'I'll drive you.' And he slammed the boot shut and walked round to the driver's seat. Over the top of the car he glanced at her. 'Better get in, or you'll never see your cases again,' he taunted with a grin, and slid in behind the steering wheel. He turned on the ignition, the car's engine started up and quickly Marina opened the door and sat down beside him, struggling to throw off a feeling of uneasiness because Vittorio had come and had apparently taken over again so that she was doing what he ordered her to do without question, as if she were mesmerised by him. He was in control and she would have to go with him.

Along the road beside the lake the branches of trees were hazy with reddish-pink swollen buds. Newly sprung grass covered the low rolling hills and on the shimmering blue-grey water of the lake a flock of white-winged dinghies were racing in a brisk breeze. High up, white and glittering, the summits of the Alps seemed to sail too against the blue sky.

'How did you get rid of Giulio?' Marina asked.

'I told him to take the day off because I would be around to keep an eye on you,' Vittorio replied.

'I'm surprised that he believed you,' she said.

'Why?'

'He got into trouble from Frankie for letting me go sailing with you. I hope he doesn't get into trouble again. I hope he doesn't lose his job.'

'You wanted to get away, didn't you?' he rebuked her sharply.

'Yes.'

'Then stop worrying about Giulio. He isn't worried about what Frankie will say to him. He's employed by Giovanni, not by Frankie.'

'Oh!' She gave him a suspicious glance but learned nothing from his face. 'I expect Frankie will be upset too when he finds out I've . . . I've . . . well, I've jilted him, I suppose,' she went on rather anxiously, remembering suddenly the stories Giovanni had told her about Frankie threatening to commit suicide. 'Do you think he'll do anything desperate?'

'Like cutting his wrists?' said Vittorio with a touch of mockery. 'No, he won't do that. Frankie is too fond of himself to ever commit suicide. I knew he threatened it before we found you and took you to see him, but now he can walk again he'll never even think of it. Possibly he'll hate you for a while because you dared to run away from him, but he'll get over you now he's on his feet again and able to chase the girls.'

'I hope you're right,' she whispered, and looked out of the car window again. With something of a shock she realised they had driven right through Montreux and that the castle of Chillon, which she had seen every day from the balcony of her room at the hotel, was quite near, seeming to float on the shimmering surface of the lake. Sitting up sharply, she looked at Vittorio.

'This isn't the way to the railway station!' she exclaimed.

'I know,' he replied coolly, and it seemed to her that the car went a little faster in the wrong direction.

'But I told you I want to go to Paris by train,' she protested.

He said nothing and the car zoomed on, following the road as it curved round the lake. They were past the castle now and Marina could see the details on the dark mountain, the rows of vines on the warm lower slopes, the sheer cliffs of grey rock above the vineyards, the sloping plateaux of green grass dotted with sheep; the rows and rows of dark coniferous trees slanting up to the snow line.

'Where are we going?' she demanded. 'Where are you taking me?'

'This road follows the Rhône estuary right into the mountains and up to the Great St Bernard Pass. We could be in Piedmont, in the north of Italy, by this evening. I know of a place, a ski-resort, where we can stay the night,' he replied smoothly.

'But I don't want to go to Piedmont,' she argued weakly. 'Please will you turn round and take me to the railway station.'

'The Val d'Aosta is very beautiful,' Vittorio continued, ignoring her protest. 'It's a series of valleys surrounded by the high peaks of Mont Blanc, Grand Paradiso and Monte Cervino—that is the Matterhorn—and it's well known for its pleasant healthy climate. I think you'll like it.'

'I'm not going there,' she said stubbornly.

'You have no choice,' he retorted, giving her a dark sidelong glance, and she felt her skin prickle with goose pimples.

She turned and looked at him, at the satanic slant of his eyebrows, at the wicked curl at the corner of his lips, and the old fear that he was some sort of messenger from the Devil flickered through her. The lines of the poem she had once read and had remembered when she had been sailing with him beat through her mind once more.

' "I will shew you where the lilies grow
On the banks of Italy," '

she quoted. 'Do lilies grow in the Val d'Aosta?'

'Not at this time of the year,' answered Vittorio without any sign of surprise as if he knew what she was talking about.

They were passing through a small town at the foot of the dark mountain. Thick-walled houses with steeply pitched roofs and overhanging eaves lined narrow cobbled streets and huddled about an old church whose square tower was topped by a tall spear-like steeple. The clock on the tower chimed the hour. It was half past noon—Marina checked her watch.

Every second that passed was taking her further away not only from Frankie but also from the direction in which she had planned to go. Cooped up in the car while it was being driven fast along the road which swept up from the town towards the Rhône Valley, she was at Vittorio's mercy. She had to go where he went. In asking for his help and in agreeing to do what he had suggested she had escaped from the Barberini web only to be ensnared in another web.

'Why are you doing this? What do you want?' she whispered.

'I want your company for tonight,' he replied.

She stared out of the window. In front of them the road zig-zagged along the green valley. Beyond the greenness were snow-covered slopes fringed with dark spindly trees.

'I see,' she said with a sigh. 'I should have remembered that you never do anything to help anyone outside your own family unless you're given something in return. I should have guessed you wouldn't help me without exacting some sort of price. I should have known better than to ask you of all people for help.'

Vittorio gave her a sharp glance, then looked quickly back at the road. They were going round a steep bend and the road hung dizzily above the valley as it climbed higher. Driving required all his care and attention. One mistake and death was almost certain if the car swerved.

'I didn't come to Switzerland to help you,' Vittorio said coldly. 'I came to take you away from Frankie. The fact that you asked me to help you only made it easier for me to remove you from his vicinity.'

'Then Giovanni did send you!' Marina exclaimed.

'He did not *send* me, but when he knew I was coming north he asked me to make sure you didn't return to Biscari with Frankie and Lucia, so I decided to kidnap you and take you away with me for the night.'

'And afterwards? Tomorrow?' she whispered.

He was quiet for a few moments as the car zoomed onwards, climbing, always climbing. Gradually the temperature dropped and Vittorio switched on the car's heater.

'Tomorrow I'll take you to Turin. From there you can travel to Paris,' he said. 'You'll be free to go wherever you like as long as you make no attempt to return to Biscari and visit Frankie. Giovanni is very grateful for the help you gave him in his ploy to get Frankie to have that operation, but he regrets he cannot allow his grandson to marry a fashion model from England.' He gave her another quick sidelong glance. 'He has already chosen Frankie's wife,' he added.

'Who is she?'

'An Italian, the daughter of a wealthy industrialist.'

'I see. Poor Frankie. And poor Bonnie,' Marina whispered.

'Why poor Bonnie?'

'She's in love with Frankie.'

'Calf-love,' he mocked. 'She'll be over it by this time next year and in love with someone else.'

'You seem to think that falling in love or rather being in love with someone is a very shortlived emotion,' she retorted challengingly.

'And so it is. It doesn't last.'

'You speak from experience, no doubt,' she said tartly.

'But of course.' His cheek creased as he grinned.

'So I suppose you approve of this outdated custom of arranged marriages?'

'Arranged marriages may be outdated in your country, but they still happen in my country and in Greece and in other countries farther east,' he replied equably. 'I neither approve nor disapprove. It is a custom which has worked well for hundreds of years.'

'I think it's a terrible custom,' she retorted. 'I would hate to have to marry someone I didn't love . . . like Emilia had to marry Eugenio Rossi.'

'What makes you think her marriage was arranged?' Surprise lilted through his voice.

'She told me once that you and she wanted to marry each other.'

'Did she?' His voice was dry. 'And why didn't we marry?'

'Because your father's business failed and you had to go to work to build it up again so you couldn't afford to marry her. She married Eugenio instead and her father approved. But she didn't love Eugenio, she loved you. She still loves you, and that's why she wants a divorce, so she can marry you now you aren't as poor as you were and can afford her.'

Vittorio was silent for a few minutes, then he said in a soft mocking voice,

'You concern yourself too much with Emilia. Soon I'll begin to think you're jealous of her.'

Marina shifted restlessly in her seat. His taunt had gone home.

'I am jealous,' she muttered. 'I'm jealous of all those women who knew you before I did.'

'Ah, yes, I remember—my amorous conquests, I think you called them,' he jeered. 'Forget them for today and tonight. None of them matter to me as much as you do at this moment.'

She turned her head swiftly to look at him. Did he mean what he was saying? It was hard to tell when all she could see was only one side of his face, a lean cheek, the crease beside his mouth, the jut of his jaw; when she couldn't see the expression in his eyes.

'I wish I could believe you,' she whispered.

'You will—tonight,' he replied. 'We'll have our time together and there'll be no more regrets.'

With her head resting against the back of the seat and her knees curled up beneath her, Marina studied what she could see of his face through her drooping lashes, remembering snatches of what Lucia had said about him.

The best of brothers and of sons. Kind and generous. A different view from the one Frankie had of him. Frankie had called him a selfish, inconsiderate swine and a womaniser. Different too from her own view of him as her daemon lover.

But suddenly she didn't care if he was everything Frankie had said he was. She didn't care about the other women in his life. She didn't care that one day when Emilia had divorced Eugenio Rossi, he would marry her. She didn't care either if he had brought her away with him to make her pay for his help by making love with him through the night. She was going to make the most of being with him, of being close to him for a short while, and even when the night was over and tomorrow came and they would part to go their separate ways at least they would have had some time together, and as Vittorio had said, there would be no more regrets, only something to remember.

CHAPTER SEVEN

SOME time later they emerged from the tunnel under the Great St Bernard Pass and passed through the Customs and Immigration post into Italy. In the dusky gold light of late afternoon they drove down to the town of Aosta and turned left on to a narrow road which twisted through one of the valleys which make up the Val d'Aosta. In front of them a high jagged peak was illuminated by the rays of the sun slanting between the mountains behind them. Brown streams, swollen by melting snows, glittered as they rushed down white hillsides to join the River Dora.

'Which mountain is that?' Marina asked drowsily. She had slept for much of the drive, only awakening when they had stopped at the border.

'Cervino. Do you ski?' asked Vittorio.

'No. I've never had the opportunity to learn. But isn't the season over?'

'In some places, yes, but up here it is often possible to ski in April. I like to come here at this time of the year when the crowds have gone. Then it's possible to ski the mountains alone.'

'You like being alone? You sail by yourself,' she said, turning to look at him curiously.

'Only if I can't find a compatible companion,' he replied.

'We're not compatible,' she mused. 'You said yourself when we first met that we strike sparks off each other.'

'By compatible I didn't mean a companion who always agrees with me or who submits easily,' he retorted. 'I like to be challenged—that is why I sail and ski for recreation. The sea and the mountains challenge perpetually.' He slanted her one of his dark insinuating glances. 'That is why I want your company for tonight,' he added softly.

'Where will we stay?' she asked, her voice shaking a little betraying the excitement which quivered through her in reaction to his suggestion.

'At an Alpine style hotel outside the resort of Breil-Cervina. There are separate chalets for guests. The owner, Severo Monelli, is a close friend of mine and was once a championship skier. Now he gives skiing instruction during the winter season and acts as a mountaineering guide in the summer.' He paused while he guided the car round another bend, then added, 'He is also my brother-in-law. My sister Sophia manages the hotel and does much of the cooking. She is a trained chef.'

'Won't they be surprised when we arrive?'

'I hope not. I phoned them from Montreux to tell them I would be arriving some time today.'

'Did you tell then I would be with you?'

'*Si*. I told them I would have a companion with me,' Vittorio replied coolly. 'There is Breil-Cervina now.'

The resort was a group of modern buildings from which lights twinkled in the violet dusk of the April evening. Behind the buildings Marina could just see the supports and cables of the ski-lifts climbing the slopes of one of the highest mountains in the Alpine Range, Monte Cervino, or the Matterhorn. Above the lower slopes sweeping ridges of snow-scattered rock rose to the towering pinnacle which gleamed softly gold as it caught the last rays of the setting sun.

They drove straight through the main street and out of the resort along a road which wound beside a stream to a two-storey building surrounded by smaller buildings, chalets with typical steeply-sloping Alpine roofs designed for snow to slide off easily.

Lights glittered from the windows of the larger building and there were a few cars parked beside it. Vittorio stopped the car at the steps that led up to a wide double front door and hooted the horn. One of the front doors was thrust open and a man wearing jeans and a thick, patterned skiing sweater came out. Vittorio got out of the car and shouted something. The man shouted back and leapt down the steps. He and Vittorio met and hugged each other.

Stiffly Marina got out of the car. The cool mountain air crisped her skin, sliced through the jacket of her suit and she shivered a little. The two men turned towards her.

'This is Marina, Severo,' said Vittorio briefly.

'Welcome, Marina,' said Severo, who was small and lithe. His lean tanned face seemed to split into two when he smiled at her and he clasped her hand in both of his. 'Come in now,' he led the way up the steps. 'Come and meet Sophia.' He pushed open the door and they entered a wide hallway furnished with low couches and armchairs, and tables. A few people were sitting there, obviously skiers, judging by their clothing. In a big hearth made from blocks of stone a log fire crackled and blazed.

From the hallway Severo led them past a stairway and through a doorway into a kitchen furnished with several cooking ranges, refrigerators and working tables with all the usual clutter of pans and cooking utensils stacked on shelves or hanging on walls. A tall woman with thick curly black hair was supervising the preparing of a meal, issuing orders to several young men and women. When she saw Vittorio she came across to him, her arms spread wide, her lips curving into a smile. She was very like him, thought Marina. Much more like him to look at than Lucia was, and much closer to him in age, about thirty-two or three.

After he had embraced Sophia Vittorio introduced Marina to her in the same offhand way he had introduced her to Severo, not mentioning her last name. Sophia's dark brown eyes assessed her curiously, but her handshake and her smile were as warm and as welcoming as Severo's had been.

'You must be tired after that long drive,' she said. Her English was much more fluent than Lucia's, but her accent was very strong. She gave Vittorio a mocking glance. 'I know how Vittorio like to drive—without stopping for food or drink. He ignores the demands of nature,' she said, laughing. 'He is supernatural and he thinks we are all the same. Come with me and I'll take you to the chalet I have prepared for you. Vittorio, bring Marina's cases, will you, to Number Four?'

The chalet was some distance from the main building and by the time she reached it Marina felt very cold and was glad to see that there was a fire blazing in the stone hearth in the small living room which was furnished with comfortable chairs and couches like the lounge hallway of the main building. The light from table lamps was soft, gleaming on wooden panelling.

'There are two bedrooms,' said Sophia, 'on either side of the bathroom. But there are no cooking facilities. We expect our guests to eat in our dining room in the main part of the hotel.' She smiled at Marina, her gaze still curious. 'Dinner will be at eight tonight. We do not have many guests this

time of the year, between seasons, so Severo and I
will have time to talk with Vittorio ... and with
you.' She paused, then added quickly, 'I have
heard of you, Marina, from Lucia. She tells me her
son Francesco is going to marry you, so I do not
understand how it is you are here with my
brother.'

'I ... I'm on my way back to England,' Marina
replied.

Sophia's eyebrows met above the bridge of her
nose in a frown of puzzlement.

'You go to England by way of Breil-Cervina?'
she exclaimed. 'I do not understand,' she repeated,
making an expressive gesture with her hands and
arms. 'But I think that perhaps Vittorio is up to
mischief. I go now to finish preparing the dinner,
and I will see you later.'

She left the chalet. Marina, still feeling cold,
moved towards the fireplace and sat down on a
leather pouffe, holding her hands out to the blaze,
thinking ruefully that the clothing she had with her
was hardly suitable for the Alps in springtime, but
then when she had set off for Sicily three weeks
ago she had no idea that she would be coming to
stay near Monte Cervino. Two weeks on a
Mediterranean island was all she had planned. The
situation had really got beyond her control.

The door of the chalet opened and she looked
round. Vittorio came in carrying her cases and his
own. He went straight over to the largest bedroom
and left the cases there, coming back to the
fireplace to crouch beside her and hold his hands
out to the blaze.

'Sophia wanted to know why I am here with you,' she said, her gaze on the thick black hair at his nape, her fingers tingling with the sudden desire to play with it. He slanted a glance at her over his shoulder.

'What did you tell her?' he asked.

'That I'm on my way to England. I didn't know what else to say, how much to tell her,' she whispered.

Turning towards her, he went down on his knees, supporting himself by putting his hands on the pouffe on either side of her. His eyes seemed to blaze into hers.

'I'll explain to her later,' he murmured.

His lips burned briefly against her throat before claiming her lips and his hands, warmed by the fire, slid under her suit jacket to curve about her breasts, the long tensile fingers crushing the soft swellings. Her lips parted in a gasp of pleasure, her eyes closed and her fingers dug greedily into his hair. For a few moments they clung together, swaying slightly, unbalanced by the fierceness of the passion that had flared so suddenly between them.

Vittorio moved away first and she almost fell off the pouffe when he ceased to hold her. Rising to his feet, he looked down at her with his mouth curving in its slight ironic smile, his eyes dancing with devilry.

'Severo is waiting for me,' he said. 'I promised to go skiing with him. It will be the only chance I have while we're here.'

'You're going now?' Marina exclaimed, disap-

pointed because the kiss had not led to more and
more and more; because it had not led to the
mysterious culmination of passion. 'But it's dark!
You won't be able to see where you're going.'

'We'll be able to see,' he replied confidently.
'There are lights all the way up the ski-tow and
soon the stars will be bright. It is always possible
to see when there is snow on the ground.'

'But what about dinner? Sophia says it is served
at eight, and I'm very hungry.'

'Then you have dinner. Severo and I will eat
when we come back,' he replied, and stepping into
the bedroom he closed the door.

By the time he came out wearing skiing clothes
Severo had arrived at the chalet looking for him.
They went off together, and feeling deserted as
well as disappointed, Marina went into the
bedroom to unpack one of her cases. She took out
her nightgown and dressing gown and the skirt
and blouse she had worn at the Barberini villa the
first night she had stayed there, thinking that with
a cardigan they would be the warmest clothes she
had with her. In the bathroom she relaxed in soft
hot water which she liberally scented with lavender
bath oil. Returning to the bedroom, she dressed,
made up her face and brushed her hair. Then,
unable to ignore the pangs of hunger any longer,
she put on her light woollen coat, tied a scarf over
her head and, wishing she had warm boots to wear
on her feet instead of sandals, she left the chalet
and hurried through the cold crisp air to the main
building.

Dinner was served in a pleasant room with a

low ceiling crisscrossed by heavy beams, and since there weren't many other guests, Sophia came from the kitchen and sat down to eat with Marina.

'Isn't it dangerous for Severo and Vittorio to ski at night?' Marina asked.

'*Si*, it is dangerous. But Severo knows this mountain well. He could ski it blindfolded, I think. And then they are both men who like taking risks—especially Vittorio. He enjoys a challenge; a storm at sea; a blizzard when he is skiing; a high mountain to climb. He likes to overcome,' Sophia replied, and looked directly at Marina, her dark eyes probing. 'You too like taking risks, I think. You would not have run away with Vittorio today, if you didn't.'

'I had no choice but to come with him,' retorted Marina. 'I had to get away from Frankie, and Vittorio said he would help me. It was his idea to come here, not mine. And he didn't have to help me if he didn't want to,' she added defensively.

'He would want to help you,' said Sophia with a sigh. 'He is attracted to you and he probably sees you as another challenge to overcome.'

'Are you trying to warn me about something?' asked Marina suspiciously.

'*Si*. I would not like you to be hurt by him.' Sophia paused, her mouth quirking a little in the same way Vittorio's did when he was secretly amused by something. 'How shall I put it?' she murmured, and looked at Marina again, sympathetically this time. 'My brother has a reputation for loving and leaving women.'

'I know—Frankie told me,' said Marina. 'And

I've wondered why Vittorio is like that. Is it because he couldn't marry Emilia Barberini when he wanted to? Is it because she married someone else?'

'No, oh no.' Sophia shook her head, smiling a little. 'It has nothing to do with Emilia. Vittorio never wanted to marry her.'

'But she told me he did,' exclaimed Marina.

'Emilia wanted to marry him,' said Sophia. 'That is something quite different from Vittorio wanting to marry her. He has never wanted to marry any woman, as far as I know, and I think that is because he hasn't found a woman who can hold his interest for long, who is sufficiently challenging.'

'Not even Gina Cortesi?' queried Marina.

'His secretary?' exclaimed Sophia, her eyes opening wide. 'What do you know about her? Have you met her?'

'No. Frankie told me she is also Vittorio's mistress.'

'*Dio mio!*' gasped Sophia, and began to laugh. She laughed so much that tears ran down her cheeks and the other people in the room turned to look at her. 'Ah, that is funny,' she said at last, mopping her eyes with a table-napkin. 'Gina is as old as my mother! She was working for the Matissi company when my father was alive and she continued to work—actually for my mother who ran the business with Vittorio's help—after my father died. She is a most virtuous, hard-working woman who would never have an illicit relationship with any man.' Sophia's eyes narrowed thoughtfully. 'What exactly did Frankie say about her?'

'He said that Emilia had probably come face to face with Gina when she went to visit Vittorio in Catania and as a result retreated to Biscari again,' muttered Marina.

'If Emilia went to Vittorio's office to see him she would meet Gina, who is very protective of his time. I expect she told Emilia she couldn't see him that day,' explained Sophia, looking amused again.

'And then Frankie said Gina was his mistress.'

'Why would he tell you a lie like that?'

'I think he wanted me to dislike Vittorio and to distrust him,' whispered Marina.

'Did he succeed?'

'Yes, he succeeded,' admitted Marina with a sigh, remembering miserably that it had been thoughts about Emilia and Gina that had caused her to resist Vittorio's lovemaking when she had been with him on the yacht.

Vittorio and Severo had not returned by the time she had finished dinner, so she sat for a while in the lounge hallway talking with some of the guests, but eventually, feeling drowsy, she decided to go back to the chalet and go to bed. She found Sophia in the kitchen, told her where she was going and said goodnight.

Outside she was surprised how light it seemed. The snow-covered slopes of the mountain glittered under the starlight and the ski-tow lights, and for a few moments she stood staring up at the slopes imagining she could see two dark figures zigzagging back and forth. But it was too cold for her to stand for long and soon she was running up the path to the chalet.

The fire had died down, so she put on more logs and sat down on the hearthrug, resting her head against the pouffe and gazing at the flames as they leapt up, thinking about Vittorio and wishing he would come soon. Gradually her head sank forward, her eyes closed and she slept.

She wakened when she felt she was being lifted. Strong arms were around her and she was being carried. She opened her eyes and saw Vittorio's jaw.

'What are you doing?' she whispered.

'Taking you to bed.'

'You don't have to carry me. I can walk,' she protested, but she made no attempt to slide from his arms.

'I expect you can, but it's much more interesting if I carry you there,' he replied with a ripple of amusement.

Soft, rose-shaded light slanted across the double bed. He put her down upon it and sat beside her. He had obviously bathed or showered, because his hair was wet and sleek except where small curling tendrils had begun to dry about his brow and ears and he was wearing only a dressing gown made from black silk which left his chest bare.

'You were away a long time,' she said.

'We went farther than we had intended,' he replied, raising a hand and weaving its fingers in her hair. 'Were you anxious?'

'No.' She smiled, that slightly mischievous, mysterious smile which had appeared on the covers of a fashion magazine. 'I had a long talk with Sophia. She told me a lot . . . about you.'

Vittorio's hand was still suddenly and his glance grew wary, but he said nothing. His hand dropped from her hair and he began to move away. Shyly Marina reached out a hand and touched his wrist. Her fingers curled about it, savouring its strength, the cool dampness of his skin.

'Where are you going?' she asked, leaning towards him urgently.

'To bed,' he replied coolly, slanting her one of his wicked glances from under down-drooping lashes. 'In the other room.' He yawned, one hand covering his mouth. 'I'm tired too.' He looked down at his other wrist, which she was still grasping. 'If you would please let go, I'll leave you,' he said.

She let go of his wrist, and sinking back against the pillows, stared at him in puzzlement, once more feeling disappointment beginning to swell in her.

'But I thought . . . I thought . . . we were going to sleep together,' she whispered. It was hard to form the words because her lips were trembling with disappointment and also because it was hurting her to trample her pride in the dust.

'I wouldn't want you to think I insisted on sleeping with you because I want something from you in return for helping you,' Vittorio replied, and bitterness edged his voice.

'I'm sorry. I shouldn't have said that to you.'

'But you did say it.'

'It was a mistake. We . . . we've both made mistakes about each other.' She gave him a quick glance from under her lashes and reached out a hand to touch one of his again. 'I'd like you to stay and ... and sleep with me,' she added shyly. 'Please, Vittorio, stay!'

'You're sure?' His expression was still wary.

'I'm sure.' And realising she would have to convince him, she sat up again and putting both hands on his shoulders offered her lips to him. 'Please kiss me,' she whispered.

He hesitated only for a second, then with a whispered oath he pressed his lips against her parted ones and slowly pushed her back against the pillow, his weight dominating her. He kissed her sweetly yet teasingly, his lips leaving hers to visit her cheek, her throat and then her breasts from which he had stroked her blouse away almost without her noticing. He kissed her savagely until her head was reeling and her body was aflame with desire. Breathless and tormented beyond reason, Marina did her best to respond, sliding her hands within his robe, rubbing the palms over the sleek smooth skin of his back, dancing her fingers lightly down his spine to caress vulnerable hollows until he groaned in an agony of pleasure and his fingers pinched her breasts bruisingly.

Once he raised his head to look at her, his eyes gleaming with mockery.

'What, no resistance?' he scoffed as if re-membering the last time they had reached this point. Her blouse and skirt had long gone, and she lay naked, her white skin rose-coloured in the lamplight.

'No, none,' she half sighed and half groaned,

and winding an arm about his neck she pulled his head down, her lips claiming his.

From then on she was lost in a warm spinning world of sensual excitement. Suddenly there was a small exquisite pain and Vittorio was in her and around her, his mouth smothering her cry as all her feelings seemed to rush together in an explosion of joy. The spinning stopped slowly. She knew where she was and what had happened, and she was drowsily content to lie there, against his warm throbbing body.

After a while he said softly as he stroked her hair,

'I think I hurt you.'

She lifted her head from his shoulder so she could see him. He was looking at her through his lashes and the tenderness in his expression made up for the small pain she had felt.

'Only a little,' she murmured shyly, touching his cheek. 'And I'm glad it was with you. I wanted the first time for me to be with you. It was wonderful!'

His lips seared her hand for a few seconds and then he was kissing her mouth again and the world was spinning again. . . .

Next morning they left the tumbled bed where they had shared so much during the night, pleasure and pain, laughter and a few tears, and bathed together in the small bathroom. Reluctantly they dressed in the clothes they had worn the previous day, packed their cases and then walked down the path through the cool mountain air to the main building of the hotel. Pink sunlight flushed the slopes of the high mountain, and as

Marina gazed up at it she remembered some lines from the poem about the daemon lover. Well, she had let Vittorio bring her to the mountain *'all so dreary with frost and snow'*, but it hadn't been to hell he had brought her. He had brought her to and had shown her *'the deep wells of delight'*, which she had read about once in another poem.

Eating breakfast was a bitter-sweet experience, because they both had to pretend nothing was different as they sat with Sophia and Severo.

'Lucia phoned, late last night,' said Sophia suddenly. 'She was very upset because Marina had not returned to the hotel.' She paused, then looking straight at Vittorio she said flatly, 'I told her Marina was here ... with you.'

'What did she say?' he asked coolly.

'She said she was relieved to know Marina was safe.' Sophia's lips twitched with amusement. 'Then she said she wasn't surprised Marina had run away with you but was glad it had happened before any official announcement had been made of Francesco's engagement to Marina. She said she would tell Francesco this morning when she visits him. She doesn't think he'll be surprised.'

Vittorio drained his coffee cup, set it down, wiped his mouth on his table-napkin and looked at Marina.

'If you are ready I would like to leave now. I have to catch a plane from Turin to Catania this afternoon,' he said coolly. 'You could fly too, to Paris from Turin ... that is if you still want to go to Paris.'

'Yes, I still want to go to Paris,' she whispered,

rising to her feet, and although he frowned at her answer, he didn't argue with her. But then he didn't invite her to fly to Catania with him, either.

There was sweet sorrow too in the drive to Turin, because although she was with him in the car for another few hours her thoughts kept leaping ahead to the parting which was to come. They would say goodbye and go their separate ways, and the chances of their ever meeting again were very remote. Marina was worried in case Vittorio kissed her because she was afraid she might break down and cling to him, but as it turned out she worried unduly. After making sure she found the right airline desk at the right terminal and that she had enough money to pay for a seat on the next flight to Paris he left her abruptly, without a word and without her knowledge. One minute he was standing beside her in the line at the airline desk, the next minute when she turned to say something to him, he had gone; had vanished into thin air, or so it seemed. Marina hoped he had gone merely to the men's room, but by the time she reached the desk and was making her reservation he hadn't returned, and she guessed, then, that he had gone for the flight to Catania which was due to take off, so he had told her, some time before the flight to Paris.

It was better this way, she told herself, better to part without saying goodbye, but all the way to Paris she sat silent and subdued, wishing Vittorio had asked her to go with him to Catania.

Three days later, having drawn a blank in Paris because Marius had been away on a tour of the

United States, Marina walked into Sylvia Trent's office in London.

'I've been wondering what had happened to you!' exclaimed Sylvia. 'Haven't heard anything about you since you left to go and have lunch with Vittorio Matissi. How did you make out with him?'

'Oh, we struck sparks off each other,' said Marina with a shrug, sliding on to the chair in front of Sylvia's desk.

'You certainly look better than you did when you were in here the last time,' remarked Sylvia. 'You've got quite a tan. Been on holiday somewhere?'

'Yes. I had a few days by the sea . . . and then went to the mountains,' replied Marina vaguely. 'Any jobs?'

'As a matter of fact there is something. I tried to get in touch with you about it last week, but your friend Annis said you were out of town. I expect you've heard of John Everly?'

'He's a designer of sports clothes.'

'Right first time. Well, he's opened a new boutique in the West End especially for women's sports clothing and *après-sports* and he's looking for someone to manage it, preferably someone with style and a knowledge of modelling, he said. The woman there now, Glenda Morton, is having to leave to go with her husband to Australia or somewhere like that. I mentioned you to John and he seemed very interested in meeting you. Would you like me to set up an appointment with him?'

'Yes, please,' replied Marina.

The interview with John Everly was successful,

and the following week she started work at the boutique, which was located in a fashionable shopping street in Mayfair. For the first few days Glenda Morton was there too, showing her how to handle the accounting side of the small business. By the end of her first month at the boutique Marina, with her natural flair for selling and modelling clothes, had increased the sales, much to her boss's delight. He raised her salary and she was able to give up sharing a flat with Annis and move into a more modern apartment nearer to her place of work.

Spring gave way to summer and the busy tourist season. The boutique flourished. Marina had little time to spare for introspection. Her new job occupied her fully five days a week and since it had brought her new friends and new admirers her social life was active, too, and although there were odd times when she thought about Vittorio she never thought about him with regret. After all, they had had some time together, they had loved each other for a day and a night.

It was the last day of July and she was in the small office at the back of the boutique making up the accounts for the month; working against the clock too because it was almost closing time, when one of the two salesgirls came in. A small Welshwoman with flashing grey eyes and abundant black hair, Stella Jones had a fiery temperament and was not above saying what she thought in language more suited to a construction site than to an elegant fashion boutique.

'It's this man. I've told him you're busy, but he

won't go away,' she raged. 'He says he's from
Sicily—wouldn't give me his name. Just said to tell
you he's from Sicily.'

'A man from Sicily?' whispered Marina, rising
to her feet. Who could have come? Frankie?
Giovanni? Could it be Vittorio?

She stepped out of the office. From behind the
tall potted plants which screened the office door
she looked into the elegantly furnished and
carpeted boutique. Vittorio was standing with his
back to her and was studying a display of beach
wear arranged on plastic models. Marina felt her
heart leap in her breast and the colour rush into
her cheeks. Taking a deep breath, she waited a
second, knowing that Stella was behind her and
watching and that Carolyn, the other salesgirl, was
moving about the salon, tidying up before they
closed. When she was sure she was calm and cool
she moved forward and said, in Italian,

'Good afternoon, sir. Can I help you?'

Vittorio swung round to face her, gave her a
quick head to toe appraising glance and stepped
towards her.

'*Comè sta,* Marina?' he said softly, and the
expression in his eyes made her knees shake.

'*Bene, grazie, e Lei?*' she whispered, her hands
clenched at her sides in case they were tempted to
reach out and touch him. In a business suit he
looked elegant and powerful. She had forgotten
how dark he was, how different.

'I am well,' he replied politely, and his gaze went
past her to Stella, then slanted sideways to
Carolyn. He looked back at her.

'Is there anywhere we could be alone?' he said softly.

'Not here. But we'll be closing soon. I . . . you could come home with me, to my apartment, if you like . . . after I've finished here.'

'I would like that,' he said simply, his eyes blazing into hers. 'How long do I wait?'

'About twenty minutes.'

'Good. I shall sit here.'

Back in the office she sat behind the desk and stared at the accounts book. The figures danced before her eyes. She couldn't concentrate. After making several mistakes she banged the book closed and pushed it into the desk drawer. Going out into the salon, she told Stella and Carolyn in crisp tones to go home. In the office again she slipped into the jacket of her linen suit, placed a wide-brimmed white hat on her head and picked up her gloves and handbag.

'Who is he, Marina?' whispered Carolyn as she dressed for the street also.

'A friend,' Marina replied coolly.

'Is it safe for you to go with him?' queried Stella, frowning. 'I mean . . . he looked at you as if . . . well, you know—as if he wants to make love to you.'

'I thought he looked at Marina as if he is *in* love with her,' said Carolyn, who was an incurable romantic. 'I wish some man would look at me like that,' she sighed. 'Goodnight, Marina.'

'Goodnight,' growled Stella. 'And be careful!'

Marina waited until they had left the boutique, then went out into the salon. Vittorio rose to his feet and came towards her.

'Do we need a taxi?' he asked.

'We'll get one on the street,' she said.

Within half an hour they were at her flat. Her fingers shook a little as she turned the key in the lock. The door swung back and they stepped inside. The door closed, and she turned to face Vittorio. They both reached out simultaneously to each other. His arms held her tightly, lifting her off her feet. His lips were hot, burning hers.

Later, much later, they lounged together side by side on the settee. Marina was wearing a silken dressing gown which she had slipped on after they had made love. In trousers, his shirt undone to the waist, his hair wildly ruffled, Vittorio was more relaxed than she had ever known him to be, and every time he looked at her he smiled.

'How did you know where to find me?' she asked.

'I went to Paris first, last week. No one knew of you at Marius Gaudin's fashion studio.' He gave her a fierce hot glance. 'I was glad, in a way, that you were not there,' he growled.

'Oh. Why?'

'I didn't like the idea of you working for that Frenchman,' he muttered obscurely. 'But when you weren't there and no one knew where you were—ah, *Dio mio*, I was frightened.'

'You?' Marina exclaimed, incredulously. 'You were afraid?'

'*Si*, I was afraid,' he repeated, his lips curving in a grin of self-derision. 'You see, I thought I would never be able to find you again. Then I came to London. I remembered the model agency, so I went there. Miss Trent told me where you were working, so I found you after all.'

His hand slid round to her nape and he tugged at her hair. She lifted her face and they kissed again and again. 'You are glad that I found you?' he whispered.

'I'm glad,' she replied, then asked hesitantly, 'How long will you be here, in London?' And she braced herself for his answer, afraid that he might say he was leaving that night or tomorrow.

'For as long as necessary,' he replied. 'I have taken leave of absence from my work. For the first time since my father died I have no responsibilities. My youngest sister is married and no longer needs my support. And my mother has gone with Lucia and Francesco to live in the States for a while.'

'Really?' She was surprised. 'I was going to ask you about Frankie. How is he? Was he very upset when he found out I'd gone away with you?'

'He was furious,' he replied with a laugh. 'And he hasn't spoken to me since. But I think he has forgiven you and realises now that for him to have married you would have been a mistake.' He gave her a sidelong glance, his mouth quirking with amusement. 'You'll be interested to know that Bonnie Spender played a big part in helping him to get over his anger at you, and she is the reason, I think, why he has decided to finish his education in the States instead of returning to England. His grandfather supported the idea and has bought a house for him in Massachusetts near the university he will attend in the fall.' He paused, then added lightly, almost gaily, 'So you see I have no mother and no sisters and no fatherless nephew to be concerned about any more. I have done my duty as a son, brother and uncle. And now I can please myself where I go and what I do.'

'I would have thought you'd have gone on an extended sailing cruise,' she said.

'I did. I had it all planned, to cruise the Greek Islands first and then to leave the Mediterranean for a while, cruise westward perhaps as far as the West Indies. I even set off, and I got as far as Biscari.' He turned to face her. His fingers twisted in a swathe of her hair, his eyes looked deeply into hers.

'Did you go alone?' she whispered, remembering she hadn't asked about Emilia yet.

'No,' he replied, his lips curving into a mocking smile. 'I had company.'

'Who?' Marina asked rather huskily, feeling jealousy twist spitefully inside her.

'My companion was the ghost of a lovely sea-maiden called Marina I had met once on the beach at Biscari and had taken sailing with me.' His grin became twisted. 'But she was poor company, insubstantial. She didn't answer back when I spoke to her. There were no arguments. No sparks were struck. And you know how realistic I am, how I prefer to make love to a real flesh-and-blood woman rather than to imagine I'm making love to her? I couldn't stand her ghostly company any longer, so I returned to Catania, left the yacht and flew to Paris to look for you. Now I am here and I've decided to stay a while, and I hope we can arrange our marriage.'

'Did you say marriage?' Marina asked cautiously.

'I did.' He frowned at her. 'You seem surprised.'

'I am.'

'You don't wish to be married to me, perhaps?' He was glowering at her now. 'Have you met someone else? Have you met someone who says he loves you and so you feel you can marry him?'

'No, no, it isn't that at all. I'm just surprised that you want to marry me,' she replied. 'I hope you don't think you have to marry me because . . . because of what happened in Breil-Cervina,' she added proudly. 'I wouldn't like you to think you have to ask me to marry you just because we'd . . . we'd had a romantic episode together.'

'How you love to throw my words back at me,' he retorted through his teeth as he glared angrily at her. 'That is not why I am asking you to marry me at all. For me marriage is a serious matter, and that is why I said I don't think it should be entered into merely for romantic love. It is a step I could never take lightly and without much thought beforehand, which is why I have never asked any woman to marry me until now. You see, according to my philosophy of life, marriage is a knot which should never be undone. Therefore it should be carefully arranged.'

'Well, it's serious for me too,' she retorted. 'And I hope you're not thinking you'll get an unpaid housekeeper by marrying me. I . . . I'm not very submissive and I could never stay at home and do the dusting while you go off sailing about the world. You would have to take me with you. I'd have to go everywhere you go if you marry me. I'm not going to be left behind.'

'Do you think I don't know anything about you?' Vittorio growled at her roughly. Leaning forward, he put his elbows on his knees and clutched his head between big hands. '*Dio mio*, I have done nothing else but think about you for the past months. I have thought about you more than any woman I've ever known. You've got into my brain and my blood and in thinking about you I've found out something new about myself. I've found out I can be as possessive and as jealous as the next man.'

He turned towards her again, his eyes ablaze, but when he spoke again his voice was soft.

'Ever since I met you I've wanted you for myself,' he admitted slowly. 'That is why I didn't want you to go to Biscari. I was afraid, you see, that you would agree to marry Francesco. But you insisted on going, insisted on staying there, even when I tried to take you away when we went sailing together, and so I believed you preferred Francesco to me after all. I could have forced you to stay with me that night . . . but that is not my way. I do not rape. I do not make love to a woman who doesn't want me as much as I want her.' His eyes glittered angrily and his breath hissed as he drew it in. 'So I took you back to Francesco and went home to Catania, to forget you.'

'I was sorry afterwards that I didn't stay with you,' Marina whispered. 'I was mixed-up, confused about you.'

'And I couldn't forget you,' he murmured. 'Then we met again in Switzerland and I knew it wasn't over for me. I could have let you go on the train to Paris, but the opportunity to have more time with you was there and I couldn't let it pass without doing something about it. So I took you to the mountains. But even there, the time was too short. You were determined to go to Paris and because I still had business and family responsibilities to attend to I had to let you go, hoping that the time we had spent together might have exorcised the spell you seem to have cast over me.' He laughed shortly. 'But it didn't. I've wanted you even more since we were together, and the idea of any other man having you has nearly driven me out of my mind. That is why I'm here, proposing marriage to you. It's the only way I can think of that I can make sure I've more right to your company than any other man has. I have come to . . . there is an English word for it. . . .' He snapped a finger and thumb together. 'I looked it up in the dictionary. It is a short word, very strange.'

'To woo?' Marına suggested, soft laughter choking her voice. He was so serious, so earnest, she couldn't help laughing at him.

'*Si*, that is it. I have come here to woo you,' he agreed, and smiled.

'But you've already done that,' she replied. 'You've been doing it ever since we met.'

'I have?'

'Yes, you've done everything you could to woo me, but I thought you were interested in only getting me into bed with you for one night. Oh, there were too many people, too many issues coming between us, confusing me—Frankie's lies about you, Giovanni's plan to get Frankie to have an operation, Emilia. But if you'd told me once that you loved me maybe I wouldn't have been confused. Do you love me?' she whispered.

'If to want to be with you all the time and to share everything with you is a definition of what you call love then I love you,' said Vittorio. Suddenly his eyes gleamed with amusement. 'Is that right? Have I said it right? Is that what you want to hear me say?'

'Yes, that is what I want to hear you say,' she replied laughingly.

'So now what are you going to say?' he challenged moving closer to her.

'I love you,' Marina murmured, winding her arms about his neck. 'And yes, I do think we should arrange our marriage to take place soon. And after we are married will you take me sailing with you?'

'*Si*, we will go sailing together, forever,' he promised, and putting his arms around her he kissed her with a reverence that left her in no doubt of his feelings about her.

Harlequin® Plus

A WORD ABOUT THE AUTHOR

Born in the port of Liverpool, England, Flora Kidd grew up to love the sea. She spent many hours with her father strolling the banks of the River Mersey, watching ships bring cargo from magic-sounding places.

While she attended university, her interest in sailing brought Flora into contact with her husband-to-be, Wilf, also a sailing enthusiast. After their marriage, he worked as a design engineer and she taught in a girls' school; from their combined earnings they saved...not for a home but for a sailing dinghy!

Eventually they moved to Scotland, where they lived in an old stone house on the Ayrshire coast. In those peaceful mountainous surroundings, with the Firth of Clyde in view, Flora began to think seriously about writing—and it wasn't long before her first novel, *Nurse at Rowanbank* (#1058), was accepted for publication.

Today the author and her family make their home in New Brunswick, one of Canada's Atlantic provinces. The Bay of Fundy has now joined the River Mersey and the Firth of Clyde as yet another maritime setting for Flora Kidd's delightful love stories.